Cracked Sky

Cracked Sky

By Ben Eads

Omnium Gatherum
Los Angeles

This is for my mother, who never stifled my imagination.

Chapter 1

Stephen Morrison held his dead daughter's doll in a shaking hand, watching rain spill from a rusted gutter. The windshield wipers fanned the water from side to side in a hypnotic rhythm.

Whomp-whomp. Whomp-whomp.

A dark gravity pulled his eyes away from the storm and toward Allie's doll. His calloused fingers massaged the little dress that Shelley had made for it like a worry stone.

Look, Daddy! Mommy says dolly and me are twins...

Stephen tilted the doll upward. Its azure eyes flipped open, as if from a nap. If he buried his nose in the crook of the neck...

Daddy, that tickles!

...it wouldn't smell anything like Allie. He smelled it anyway. Cheap plastic filled his nostrils. A sweet strawberry smell hid below it and tickled the hairs in his nose. No matter how many pills he took, memories of the good times, before the wreck, was all the projector in his mind played. A sob welled up in his chest, shaking him as if he were at the mercy of an angry sea. It begged him to stop fighting the waves and just let go. For a brief moment, he longed for his handgun.

Who loves you, Allie-bear?

He hugged the doll and pressed its cold cheek to his. But it couldn't hug back.

You do, Daddy!

It would never hug back. It wasn't Allie. It would never

be Allie. Still, he placed his thumb on its chest and waited for a heartbeat that would never come.

The clock inside the car warned he would be late for his appointment with the shrink if he didn't move now.

Stephen wiped his tears with the doll's dress and reluctantly placed it in the passenger seat. He arranged the skirt of the dress so it covered her knees.

Let's buckle you in, Allie-bear.

He turned the car off and pulled the keys out of the ignition. Stephen opened the door and stepped into the rain, losing himself in the places between the droplets. The wind bent him like the willow trees on the side of the road as he walked toward the doctor's office.

He reached for the doorknob with a hand that used to be there and bumped what was left of his right shoulder into the doorway. The pain rippled through his thin, frail body like a pebble dropped by a child in a pond.

A numb hand rubbed at his nub which only intensified the effect. Pins and needles danced on a limb that became a painful memory.

I'm going to faint.

"Mr. Morrison?" Her soothing voice was distant, underwater. "What are you doing out here in the rain? You don't even have an umbrella."

Stephen's fingernails drew little red crescents on his palm.

"I'm sorry, Doctor Sullivan."

Daddy, can you get my dolly?

"Let's go inside and get you dry, okay?"

He nodded, wiped away tears and followed her inside.

Chapter 2

"Can you take me back to that moment, Stephen? What stands out?" Dr. Meagan Sullivan jotted notes in her file.

Thunder rumbled outside, shaking the walls.

I need my prescriptions refilled. Please...

"Well, I just keep telling myself that what happened... it could have been anyone. I mean, my brother Josh was right behind us. They have *two* children." Stephen cleared his throat, snorting back tears. He stared out his psychiatrist's window into the gray sky and was pulled toward its vacuous center. "I guess what they say is true."

"What's that?"

"That everything we look at is a mirror." His dry tongue licked cracked lips. "Anyway, it's the randomness of it...I can't..."

Tears pattered like Allie's footsteps across the leather recliner, as if in a faint, ghost-like pool.

"Stephen, if you don't feel comfortable going back there *yet*, that's okay."

I can't believe I'm doing this.

"I...think I can."

"Let's give it a go, huh?"

He took a deep breath and exhaled. "There we are at the intersection. Shelley was singing to Allie in the back-seat trying to calm her tantrum. Over and over, and over again...it's like a movie stuck on replay. I can't...I can't remember what Allie asked me. Why Shelley was so upset."

Can we hurry this up?

"That's okay. Please understand, this is normal behavior given your injuries. Especially head trauma. Do you remember *anything* after that?" Doctor Sullivan brushed a stray lock of red hair behind her ear.

"The red light was taking forever. I had my hand out to Allie. She dropped her doll at some point. I saw it out of the corner of my eye on the floorboard behind us. I picked it up and handed it back to her. I heard Shelley scream, and there was this weird sound...melodic almost. Then the ice cream truck comes toward us and just cuts the car into..."

His face twitched as the pain came back: The windshield shearing his arm off; his head breaking through the window and slamming into steel at sixty miles an hour; Allie screaming his name before...

This is why, bitch. Thanks.

"You're doing fine." Doctor Sullivan removed her glasses. They reminded him of old actresses and bad movies. She placed the tip in her mouth.

"I can still feel it." Stephen raised the arm that used to be there. "My physician says they're phantom pains. The "pins and needles effect." But when I pushed her back into the car-seat... those little fingers wrapped around my pinky and they *squeezed*." Stephen wiggled an invisible digit. "They squeezed. God, I can still feel it. And that... *fuck*...that piece of shit! *He's* still alive. He's in a coma, but he's still alive." Stephen shook his head, letting out a nervous laugh. "And you know what? He just may walk out of there. He just may."

The cloud moved closer and swelled, its center a deep pool of oblivion. The pressure squeezed his head again. His vision turned hazy. He could feel vomit inching its way up his esophagus.

"Stephen, grieving is a process." She leaned forward and handed him tissues.

Stephen composed himself the best he could.

"Anger is perfectly natural. It plays a crucial part in the process of healing. It's okay to feel the way you do. We just need to work on moving forward, okay?"

His heart skipped a beat and the world went black. His fingertips played with the stitches above his left ear and a faint electricity of phantom nerve impulses flared around his healing shoulder joint.

"A four-year-old dies, and a drunk driver lives?"

"I'm sorry, Stephen."

"Do you have children? You look young enough. What if it had been you?"

"I am so sorry, Stephen. I apologize. If you're not ready to go there, then let's back off. How are the anti-depressants working?"

Stephen bit down on his lower lip until he tasted pennies.

"It numbs it, that's all."

"How about the pain?"

"Bad. Real bad. Still. And I find myself reaching for my wife, and she's reaching for a bottle."

"How *is* Shelly? Has she gone back to work at the hospital? She hasn't been here with you for counseling. I'm very concerned for you both. You're a family unit."

"A family?" Stephen let out another nervous laugh. "Is that what I'm supposed to call it?"

"How bad is it at home? Would you like to talk about that?"

Chapter 3

Stephen rounded the corner of his street and came to a slow stop. His hands shook so badly he dropped his tranquilizers and painkillers.

This is not my beautiful house.

The whomp-whomp of the windshield wipers stopped. He reached for Allie's doll...

Which is nothing but memories and pain. I need...

...but picked up his pill bottles instead. He opened them and swallowed three of each, waiting for their sweet release.

A train's siren jabbed his eardrums with toothpicks. As it passed, a low rumble followed, shaking the car and rattling the change in the cup-holder.

Did I just hear that? The track's been tore up since...

He stepped out and lumbered his way to the front door.

This is not my beautiful life.

The key fumbled in the deadlock. The rusted mechanism squeaked in protest. It was just a little off; much like what it protected inside.

This is not my beautiful wife.

He walked into the empty hallway and breathed in the peanut butter and jelly mixed with cigarettes smell of home.

"Shelley!"

It was just *Shelley,* now. No more *Honey,* or *Love.* And by no means *Shell.* The thought pained him. It was too close to...

The truth.

"Shelley."

Something danced in the corner of his left eye and he saw her frail form nestled under the window, hidden by the gloom. Wide and vacant eyes stared, fixed on nothing.

"Shelley?" he waved his hand in front of her face.

"I'm going to live with my parents for a while. I can't take this. I'm done."

Time slowed as he placed his hand on the wall and lowered his head between his knees and breathed.

Stephen cleared his throat, tasting the residue from the pills as they slid down his throat. "You're being childish. You know that, right?"

"No. *Childish* is our therapist calling and asking me why I drink so much, when you're the one that's passed out every—"

"I...I had to tell her."

"We've...I can't believe I'm saying this, but, I need you to be a man. I know you're suffering, but we're—"

"Oh! Hello, Shelley's father! We weren't expecting you, but come on in!"

"I can't talk to you right now." She got up and walked down the hall.

I can't believe what I just heard myself say...

"Shelley?"

Stephen heard her slippers come to a stop on the hardwood floor.

"What?"

"I found her doll. You know, the one you made the dress for. It's in the car...and for the life of me, I can't touch it anymore. It's...I'm done, too." Stephen felt a pang in his chest, like someone had just hit the pause button.

Stephen watched her walk back into the room, and for a moment, he thought he saw understanding in her face. Or pity.

Does it really matter which?

"How do you think I feel? I lost my Allie-bear!" Tears spilled and Shelley's body shook like a tree in a hurricane. "She's gone. And the more I stay...the more I stay here, the more it...it eats at me....like some starved animal."

"Please. Can we call a truce?"

"You were right. I'm a hypocrite. But you have no right to tell her that!" Shelley sobbed, pointing her finger at him.

"Please forgive me. I'm...I'm doing the best I can. We both are, right? I knew it would be hard, but this..."

Shelley nodded and approached.

"I'm sorry, too," Stephen said, as he stood.

He embraced her shaking body, and for the first time in two weeks, he felt a tingle of strength.

The feeling left as quickly as it came.

Their storms coalesced into a crescendo that scraped his eardrums. When it passed, she fell asleep on his chest. He closed his eyes and followed her.

~

Stephen stood chest-high in the ocean with Allyson in his arms, feeling the great ebb and flow of the tide. He felt microscopic compared to the azure forever that kissed the sun. His feet sank a little deeper with each breath of the Atlantic.

"Daddy, I'm scared."

"You're in my arms, okay? Nothing bad can happen to you, Baby." Stephen kissed her forehead. Her fear faded as her blue eyes stared into the great yawn. "And when you're old enough, you'll get to go scuba-diving with us, yeah?"

Reluctantly, she grinned.

A scream bounced between his eardrums.

"Stephen!"

Allyson gasped and he felt her tiny arms encircle him.
"What is it, Sweetie?"

He followed her eyes and looked behind him. Shelley stood at the edge of the beach, waving her arms. Warmth poured over their bodies as he clutched Allie tight.

"Mommy needs us. Wanna go see Mommy?"

"Yeah."

"Let's go, Bugga-boo."

He pulled at his feet and the ocean's floor yanked back. The coming wave rolled closer, rising up, turning his bowels to ice. Commands from his brain to move his feet failed.

A siren wailed like an air raid—a warning.

It's coming.

"I can't. Help!" Was all he could muster as he enveloped little Allie, placing her face over his shoulder, closing his eyes.

"Don't look, Baby. You don't want to see this."

The air raid squelched like an engine throwing a piston rod. Invisible metallic spikes entered his ears, seeking softer tissue.

Don't pass out. Allyson need me.

The wave crashed over them, bending him back like a blade of grass in the wind as debris raced across his body.

I forgot to take a breath. Did Allie?

The wave yanked them forward. Feet sank deeper, his knees straining at the force. A tendon snapped like a guitar string. Fireworks went off behind his eyes.

He opened his eyes and watched the sun get brighter as Allie struggled in his arms.

I can't breathe.

The warm, silken waters turned cold and harsh as they pulled at little Allie-bear. Every movement slowed as he turned to ice. The siren became a telephone ringing.

Stephen awoke as if a shotgun had been fired by his ear.

He took in gulps of air, feeling the grip of that tiny hand.

I can still feel the wave.

The sound of the phone was now clear and crisp; a sound he loathed, burrowing into his head like a greedy termite.

Shelley snorted, and twitched. Stephen shook his head, laid her carefully against the couch, and picked up the phone.

"Hello?" His voice was groggy and his throat felt like it was filled with Styrofoam.

"Stephen! Thank God. How are you, buddy?"

"Frank. What's wrong?"

"Nothing. We're calling to see how you and Shelley are doing. I hope I didn't catch you at a bad time?"

Stephen's sigh filled the long pause.

"Look, I just wanted to let you know that we understand your situation. Now, don't worry about bereavement leave, okay? I talked to the higher-ups and you're cleared for another month. God bless the Family Medical Leave Act, my friend."

Stephen tried to speak but the Styrofoam expanded.

He hung up the phone and barely made it to the toilet and vomited into the sink. After the dry heaves passed, he stared at his emaciated body. At the dark sockets his eyes called home. The stubble across his face that had turned white in just under a week.

Stephen splashed cold water on his face. He turned the faucet on full-blast and stuck his head under its cool, soothing rush. Looking up, this time, he saw the face of his father. Pills? Check. Alcohol? Check. Ready to say fuck it?

Magic 8 Ball says: Ask again later.

He felt unsteady, like sand was shifting under his feet. Stephen leaned forward, elbow on the sink, and turned the water off.

He grabbed a towel and dried his face as he listened

for Shelley. He stepped out of the bathroom and peeked into the living room. She lay on the couch, her chest slowly rising and falling.

Good. She needs it.

He turned and tripped on one of Allie's wooden spelling blocks.

Biting his lip against the urge to scream, he hopped up and down, his hand massaging his foot.

"Fuck," he managed and leaned against the wall feeling the throb in his head pound away. His sight came and went with each loop. Thud-thud. Thud-thud.

Allie's Blocks were scattered all down the hallway. Letters, shapes and colors dotted the wooden floor. Stephen moved the majority of them with his foot and found himself in Allie's doorway.

Am I really ready for this?

He took a deep breath and entered with his toes maneuvering through the debris.

Out of habit, he leaned forward with his right shoulder and realized there was only air. He cursed himself and flipped the light switch on with this left hand.

He shielded his eyes from the intensity as haunting thoughts swam through his gray matter. Memories came in flashes while he searched for Allie's red toy box.

Look what I painted for you today, Daddy.

The porcelain doll Grandma bought her for her last birthday sat atop it, grinning.

Mommy says it's her favorite! See, Daddy? This one is you. This is Mommy, and this is a kitty-cat.

Stephen picked the doll up like a treasure and placed it on her bed. Lifting Allie's toy box, he began putting blocks inside.

Why, Daddy? Mommy said I could have a kitty-cat! I've been a good girl all year, Daddy!

"I'm sorry, Baby. I'm so very sorry, my Allie-bear."

He felt the storm coming again and sat down in anticipation. Pins and needles returned along with a deep itch that he couldn't scratch.

His arm rubbed at fevered eyes, as he watched what he *felt* happening. One of Allie's wooden blocks hung in the air. Stephen imagined himself letting go of it, and it dropped. He looked next to the box, where a limb that didn't exist anymore had arranged a few of them.

H E

Stephen imagined himself picking up another block, trying to feel for it. Nothing. He shook his head and ice spread across his skin.

What's happening to me?

He closed his eyes in protest as more tears fell. Another surge went through his arm.

I love you, Allyson. I love you so much.

He rocked himself back and forth until the worst of it subsided. He went to stand up and fell right back down when he saw it: HELP ME DADDY

"Stephen. What are you doing?"

"Jesus, you scared me."

Don't look at the blocks.

"Your brother has been banging on the door for—"

"Josh is here?"

"I didn't want to answer. I'm not feeling like it."

Don't look down.

"Okay," he said and stood to embrace her, but she backed away.

"I'm going to watch some TV. If the hospital calls, my cell has contact numbers for the nurses that can cover for me."

She walked into the bedroom and closed the door.

Stephen turned and had to force his eyes open. The blocks were gone. He sighed, feeling the weight lift.

Chapter 4

Through the peephole, Stephen saw the top of Josh's bald head in the window. He unlocked the dead bolt and opened the door. The smell of pot smoke wafted in making him nauseated.

Josh's jowls were flushed red and his green sweater rippled over his girth. "For God's sake, how many weeks is it going to rain?" In the center of his little, pudgy face, his nose twitched like a mouse. "You have to let me come over and clean. This smell is foul. What is that smell, anyway? It's like rank peanut butter."

"I don't know and I don't care."

"Here," Josh placed the crock pot and Tupperware atop a small, dusty table in the foyer. "I don't have to be a private investigator to know that you guys need this. And I'll bring more tomorrow."

"Please don't start."

"Wait. Oh my God," Josh said as he lifted his foot from the sticky floor. "This is worse than I thought."

"It's not *that* bad. C'mon." Stephen motioned for them to walk down the hallway.

As they walked, Josh gasped. "No offense, but I've seen a few crack houses on the news...and they look *much* better than this. I can't even see the kitchen counter, and the living room looks like a fort that kids would make. There's blankets...cereal on the floor..."

Oh, shut the fuck up!

Stephen held up his hand. "Stop! Stop. Please. Not now."

Josh held up his. "Hey, peace, bro. I'm just saying."

Stephen opened the liquor cabinet. He pulled out a bottle and two dirty glasses. "I need this more than you can possibly imagine."

"Oh!" Josh said, producing a joint, "We have good news to celebrate, bro. *Very* good news. This will help, my man."

"You know that shit makes me wanna puke. No thanks."

Josh placed the joint behind his ear. "No worries. Have you seen the news?"

"No, what happened?" Stephen opened the bottle and splashed liquid courage into each glass. "It's probably best we go outside. Shelley isn't feeling well."

As Stephen closed the French doors behind them, a half-moon illuminated a rainy, summer night. A chorus of tree frogs competed with the cicadas. Lilac flooded Stephen's nose. Lightning flashed in the distance.

Rain hit the steel roof like a snare drum. They sat down, sipping at the whiskey. The scent of it was accented by the orange blossoms that hung above them.

"So, what's so important?"

"That...that piece of shit who caused the accident, he's dead. Due to some interesting complications...he flat-lined sometime this afternoon. I was in the middle of filming a guy for insurance fraud when Darlene called me and gave me the news."

Like Stephen's thoughts, time slowed to a crawl. An anger he had never felt before erupted inside him, sobering him up. Stone sober.

He can't get off that easy. Fuck!

Stephen reached under his lawn chair, pulled a cigarette from the pack and lit it. His right eye twitched.

"He's dead?"

"Yeah, it looks like you and Shelley don't have to worry

about going to court."

Lightning flashed and Stephen felt the thunder shake his drink.

"I don't give a *fuck* about that. He should have fuckin' suffered."

"He *did* suffer."

Stephen spat out his whiskey. "How?"

The rain intensified, as if the entire sky just opened. Stephen leaned forward and craned his ear to listen above the din.

"Being a private investigator has its perks, bro. I did some digging and get this; the guy who lived under Darrell called the apartment complex last week because of a water leak. They show up, and it's coming from Darrell's apartment."

Stephen's heart raced. Somewhere in the distance, a loon cried out. It echoed across the lake, reverberating in his head.

Oh, this better be good!

"Anyway, it took the apartment manager opening his door, and what they found...this guy wasn't Donald Trump rich, but rich as hell. Eccentric, too. The guy had a whole library of books on the occult and furniture made out of human skeletons. But the media kept focusing on a note they found in his bedroom that was dated the *day* of the accident. It made him out to be some kind of terrorist...it was a manifesto of sorts."

I need more pills...this is too much.

"It said that he was looking for a place where reality was thin. According to the note, he found it. Whatever he was smokin,' I'd love to have some of it."

The sound of a tree falling down the street made Stephen jump in his seat.

"That's it? What else? Give me something good." Stephen downed what was left of his whiskey.

"Just the usual stuff. Loner. Barely knew anyone."

"If he was rich, why was he driving an ice cream truck? Was he a pedophile?" The storm forced the rain sideways. It sprayed across his face, his feet.

"Eccentric? Yes. Pedophile? No. They found nothing. And trust me, if they did, they would have been all over it."

Stephen felt the air being sucked from his lungs.

"It gets better."

"I really hope so."

"Here's the kicker, they found a single children's toy block lodged in his throat. Now, the press doesn't know that. That's between us."

Stephen could only stare, jaw agape, his consciousness spiraling. His heart beat in his fingertips.

Help me, Daddy.

Rain turned to hail, assaulting the tin roof like a machine gun.

"Someone managed to jam the damn thing down his throat," Josh said and finished his drink. "And, if it weren't for the cameras in the Intensive Care Unit, we'd be suspects talking to the Police. From what I heard, there's nothing there. My money's on his "missing" wife. Probably took their daughter and got the hell out of dodge. Creepy shit, bro."

"Wait! Do you hear that?" Stephen said.

"Yeah, sounds like the goddamn blitzkrieg! Look out! Here come za Germans!"

"No, not that. Listen. You don't hear that?"

"Bro, you're freakin' me out here, and I'm sober. What is it?"

"It sounds like a train. You know, the one that used to run by the lake? But they shut it down after it derailed...it hasn't run in years."

"Uhhh...nope. Don't hear it."

"I guess it's just been a really, really tough day. I think I need to go to bed." Stephen stood and patted Josh on the shoulder. "I deeply appreciate the news, though."

"I'll be back again tomorrow with some home-cooked food for you guys, okay?"

"That sounds good." Stephen opened the French doors and they stepped inside.

It's just the head trauma. Yeah, that's it.

"What the hell is that smell?" Josh peered in the kitchen sink. He wretched.

Stephen looked over Josh's shoulder. "They're just maggots. I haven't had time to clean up."

"Okay. I am coming over to clean. This...there's no excuse for this." Josh backed out the room toward the front door.

Please, please leave. Where the hell are my pills?

"Josh, I don't feel well at all. Tomorrow. We'll discuss it tomorrow."

Stephen twitched from withdrawal.

"I'll call you tomorrow afternoon, before I stop by." Josh hugged him.

"Thanks."

Stephen locked the front door after Josh. He took a deep breath and exhaled.

You're not going crazy. You've never been crazy. It's just...a side effect from the wreck.

Stephen pulled his plastic pill bottles out of his pocket. Struggling to open them with one hand, he dropped them.

They rolled down the hallway and stopped in front of Allie's bedroom.

It didn't happen. You're not going crazy. Just look.

Stephen approached the doorway as if it were a ticking time bomb. Despite the AC, sweat poured off him. This time, it wasn't the withdrawals.

Look!

He picked up the painkillers, and opened the bottle

with his teeth. His fingers dug in for a few of his friends. He dry-swallowed them.

Just a few blocks away, a train that hadn't passed through town in over sixty years shook the plates in the kitchen sink, rattling the windows.

What are you afraid of?

Stephen turned the light on in Allie's room.

HELP ME DADDY

~

Stephen awoke on the couch, shaking. His lungs fought to keep what air they had, and stuttered seeking more, like a car running on fumes. Thoughts raced along countless highways in his head. He swung his legs from under the covers and flinched at the cold wood floor.

Stephen took a deep breath and stood. The head-rush tottered him like a wind-up toy as he walked down the hallway toward the bathroom where his little friends lived in their bottles.

"Where are you, you little bastards?" He fumbled through old prescription bottles.

"Honey, are you okay?" Shelley called from the kitchen.

Where the fuck are they?

"Shelley! Have you seen my pills?" Stephen marched into the kitchen.

"Umm...yeah! They're here in the kitchen by the faucet... You're shaking."

"Yeah, good morning to you too, Love."

Stephen opened the tranquilizers and painkillers. He placed three of each side by side, grabbed an ashtray and began to grind them to a fine powder.

"What are you doing?"

"Huh?"

Grind fuckers, grind!

"I asked, what are you doing?"

"I'm a...It's the same amount I usually take, I'm just...I found a way for them to hit me quicker."

"Hit you quicker?"

"Yeah. Where's my straw?" His heart raced. "Have you seen a little straw piece that I cut off so I can...so I can, you know." He found a face painted with fear staring at him.

"*No*. I haven't."

"Okay. No big deal." He leaned over, covering his left nostril and inhaled until he felt the chalk drip down his throat. His tongue lapped up the rest.

A train's siren screeched.

Feeling dizzy, Stephen clutched the edge of the kitchen sink as it rolled past their house, rattling the pipes under the sink.

Shelley sighed and folded her arms. "I think we need to talk about this."

"Yeah, sure." He chose the seat furthest from her. "What's up?"

"We're in this together. I know what you're going through." She reached across the table.

Stephen withdrew his hand.

The sigh she made scraped his withdrawal-stricken brain like nails across a blackboard.

"But you need to stop. You need to stop abusing the pills. I understand, but after a while— Stephen you're always asleep! And...and the alcohol is a deadly mix. I lost count of how many times I found you and your breathing...your breathing was *very* labored."

Kick in already!

"Can't we deal with one problem at a time? Huh? I mean... sleep? You want to bring that up? Do you know what I see every time I close my eyes? Do you?" Stephen pounded the table so hard that the salt and peppers shakers jumped a few inches and landed, clinking like raindrops off the rusted gutter.

"Talk to me. Don't fight me. Please? I'm trying to help you."

"I just need a few minutes, okay? I just got up. I'm trying my best. But right now...I can't..."

A hint of euphoria cascaded through him, lulling the shakes and pain as the world began to twist, distort.

Soon, all will be well.

"Stephen?" Shelley repeated.

"Yeah? What?"

"You fell asleep, *again*."

"Oh..." He wiped the drool from his mouth. "I'm exhausted. I'm sorry."

"You're *scaring* me. I've never seen you like this. You need to slow down. Just a little. Look, let me help you, okay?"

"I want to say that you don't know what it's like. But you do. You do. Like I said, why don't we deal with one problem at a time, is this really too much to ask?"

"I love you. I'm trying to help you—"

"Do you have any idea what kind of stress I'm under? How many times do I have to say it? *I just fucking woke up!*" The chair skidded across the tile as he pushed back and stood. The sound bore into the hole in his head Shelley's sigh had created. "I just came in here for my pills and...and I just need to clear my head. How about we put the spotlight on *you*. How's that? Why don't we do that!"

"Please, calm down. You don't have—"

"Then just let me...just let me breathe, okay? I just need a few minutes, goddammit."

Stephen stomped down the hallway then stopped. He walked back into the kitchen, picked up his pills and walked back into their bedroom and shut the door.

A bladder on the verge of bursting forced him to rush into the bathroom. He made it just in time.

His ethereal arm popped and crackled to life and pinched off the stream, poking his bladder with a knife.

"Fuck!"

Stephen tried to grab his arm in vain. He grabbed his penis with his left hand which only tightened the grip, and the pain.

It's going to burst, it's going to burst.

"Please!"

A flutter of memories panned across the theater of his mind until he found the one of him swinging Allie at the park.

Push, Daddy, push!

When she kicked out, the seat hit him between the legs...

The flow returned and footfalls echoed down the hall-way.

"Stephen!"

He held his right arm out and wiggled the digits, affirm-ing his control.

"What the hell?" Stephen said.

"Are you all right?"

"My arm...it came to life on its own."

"I know," she said after a long pause. "It's the phantom pains, like the doctor said."

"No, I mean it hurt me. It just came to life and it tried to hurt me."

"What do you mean, it hurt you?"

"It grabbed my junk and pinched it shut. I thought I was going to blow a gasket."

"Come here." She embraced him. "We're going to make it through this. I know we will. And don't think for a moment that all of this is on you. I hurt, too. In just dif-ferent—"

"What, Love?"

Shelley grabbed her throat and tried to breath; her eyes swelled until they bulged.

Her throat looked like it had a dent. Shallow clicking sounds escaped.

What the...

"Are you okay?" He cupped her cheek in his palm. "That's it. Breathe, Baby, breathe. There you go."

When the coughing passed, her face was as red as fire. She placed her hands on her knees, leaned forward and inhaled.

"Are you okay?"

"Yeah," she panted.

Stephen rubbed her back and ran his fingers through her amber hair. The touch reminded him of other times, good times. Then the pain that came with it took its place.

"You had me worried, Shell. You sure you're okay?"

"I think I had a panic attack. I just couldn't breathe. And it was cold. My throat, it was cold." Her hand rubbed her throat. "I've been trying to warm it up."

"Do you want a tranquilizer?"

"No, I'm good," she inhaled deeply, "whoo! I need water," she said, turning to leave.

A faint ripple ran like hot candle wax down his absent appendage.

"Hey!" She turned, her mouth agape. "What the hell was that?"

"What was *what*?"

"So...the Easter bunny pushed me?"

She pointed at him; her lean muscles taught. "Stay. The. Hell. Away."

He'd never seen her so bold, on fire.

"I don't know what you're talking about!" Steven said.

"Stay away from me!" She backed out the bedroom as if walking on glass. "Let's just keep our distance."

"I...Shelley, please, just listen to me."

"You pushed me!"

"I didn't have any control. You saw it! It's some kind

of stupid fuckin' side effect from the wreck." Stephen watched what was left of his life trickle away like the rain drops on their bedroom window.

Shelley stormed out of the room.

Quaking, he crawled to the bathroom. Stephen opened his pill bottles, popped two more into his mouth and swallowed them dry. He scooted on his ass over to the toilet and pulled his legs up against his chest, embracing them with the only arm he had. In the distance, a train's siren echoed.

Emotions carried him to a place he had found only in his nightmares: A place that held souls like treasure and children as dolls. He leaned over on his side, in the fetal position. Written in blood on the tile floor: WHY DID YOU PUT ME HERE DADDY?

Chapter 5

"Stephen, wake up!"

"Jesus...Christ. What's wrong?" He yawned and rolled over on the bathroom floor, trying to shrug off the recurring nightmare of their trip to the beach. He steadied himself and managed to walk to the bedroom.

"Look!" she pointed the remote at their television, turning up the volume: *Yesterday evening, Darrell Peakman— the drunk driver responsible for taking the life of a local four-year-old girl—passed away. Doctors said the injuries he sustained during the accident played a large role in his death. Mr. Peakman's wife, Anne has been missing for weeks and was not available for comment. You know, Jennifer, I can only wonder what that little girl's parents are thinking right now.*

"The fucking vampires will probably call to find out." Stephen stumbled back into the bathroom. He popped three painkillers and two anti-anxiety pills in his mouth and drank from the faucet. The chalky residue that slid down his parched throat soothed him. A low rumble vibrated the bones in his legs, as he felt a train pass by.

"Stephen, come here!"

"I'm here, Baby. What's going on?" he said, and almost brought his pills back up when he saw her. Her eyes bulged out of her beet-red face. Her jaw trembled.

Should I offer her one of my pills?

He sat on the side of the bed.

Shelley moved toward the television.

"He's dead! I mean...I can't see how I could have missed this. But, he's *dead*."

"I know. Josh told me last night." He motioned for her to join him.

"What?" Her gaze seared through him. The heat coming off her was oppressive, accusing. "When?"

"Last night when he came over."

"Why didn't you wake me up?" She crossed her arms. Her eyes glowed like cigarettes, flaring with each inhale of the stale air between them.

"What's wrong? I was going to tell you."

"But what?" She moved closer, grinding her teeth as her chest heaved with each breath.

God...I hate that sound. And you know it, Shelley.

"Well, you haven't had a decent night's rest in I don't know how long. I'm sorry, okay? Just, please, calm down. Here, sit beside me and let's *talk* about it." Stephen motioned for her to join him again. "I just woke up and my medication hasn't even kicked in yet."

"You're sorry? So, because I don't sleep enough you—"

"Shelley, what's wrong?"

"What's *wrong?*" She threw the remote at him. The side of it clipped his head and the world winked out for a moment.

"What's wrong is that you knew this. You *knew* this! And you didn't even wake me up? And you say it's because I don't get enough sleep? Last night you had an episode! You can't even control yourself!"

"I thought it would be best if we got some sleep and talked about it later."

She turned from him and started throwing on her clothes.

"That is our goddamned daughter! And you...you know what?" She grabbed her purse, car keys, and pointed at him. "How dare you. How fucking *dare* you!"

Shelley stomped down the hallway and slammed the front door behind her. She opened it again and slammed it even harder.

"Fuck!"

The scream seared his throat. It was a pain he welcomed. He leaned over, grabbed the phone and dialed his brother. Listening to the dial tone, he watched the rain that came a month ago continue to pelt the world.

~

"I don't know why I have to keep opening the door for you. You have a set of keys." Stephen closed the door behind them and locked it.

Josh wore the same clothes he had on yesterday, and there was a funk from him in the air. What hair he had left stood up as if he had been electrocuted.

"You want a shot?" Stephen kicked clothes and empty liquor bottles out of the way.

"Wow! You did some partying last night, bro." Josh walked behind him into the kitchen. "And I see my assistance is needed now more than ever. You didn't even touch the dishes."

Stephen pulled the whiskey bottle and the same glasses they used last night off the shelf.

"No thanks, bro. I have to get back to work. I'm not trying to come down on you, but this has to be said...you shouldn't be mixing alcohol with prescription drugs."

"If you knew what I went through last night, you'd shut your fat, fuckin' mouth."

Stephen regretted his words as soon as they came out.

Josh held up his hands in surrender. "Hey, peace, bro. I'm just really concerned, okay? What the hell happened, anyway?"

"Sorry I snapped."

"After all you've been through. No worries."

Josh began to pick up the empty liquor bottles and place them in the garbage can.

All the fight in Stephen left him and despair took its place. He felt alone in an elevator that was free-falling to the bottom.

Stephen poured and slammed back another shot.

"Shelley left me."

"*What?* I don't understand. What happened?" Josh looked like he was trying to solve the world's hardest math problem.

"Come on, let's have a seat on the back porch."

Stephen opened the French doors and stepped outside.

"You sure you don't want a drink?"

"No, I'm good. But, we'll see how it goes."

Josh joined him. His lawn chair squeaked as he sat down.

The familiar chorus of cicadas and tree frogs filled Stephen's ears. The steady beat of the rain made his head throb.

"So, tell Dough-boy what happened."

"I had the worst nightmare, and Shelley wakes me up pointing at the television." Stephen shrugged the only shoulder he had. "She's turned into her mom." He laughed and took a sip of his drink. "Just like her goddamned mom. I mean, I could actually see her mom in her eyes."

Stephen placed his glass on the arm of the lawn chair to swat at a mosquito.

"I'm so sorry, man."

"It's them! Her parents have been," Stephen clawed at the air, "ripping at her to leave me ever since, well, you know. They blame me. So does Shelley."

"Maybe if I called her? Talked to her?"

Did I take too many pills?

"Don't you understand? I'm responsible for World War I *and* World War II," Stephen held up his fingers, "and

Justin fucking Beiber!"

Stephen reached under the chair and pulled out a cigarette, lit it, and exhaled slowly, relishing the bite in his chest.

"You're not a Belieber? Man...that's fucked up," Josh said, snickering.

Stephen laughed. And just for a moment, he felt like a bird. He felt free.

The feeling left as quickly as it came.

"See! I knew I'd get you to laugh, bro."

"Ha, ha."

Stephen took a deep pull off his cigarette and blew smoke at Josh's face.

Josh coughed, fanning it away.

Stephen cleared his throat. "My handgun. That's what I need."

"Okay, now you're scaring the fuck out of me."

Stephen couldn't help but let the tears fall. He actually felt good when they came, like a cloud releasing acid rain.

Josh placed his hand on Stephen's shoulder. "You listen to me, okay? No more of that talk. It's gonna work out. I'll call Shelley and we'll go from there. Until then, I'm not leaving you here alone, bro."

"Thanks," was all Stephen could manage between sobs.

"She'll take a vacation, but that's all she'll do. You guys have been through too much. She's won't give up on you. After I call her, you'll see."

"She's all I have left," Stephen muttered over and over. I'm nothing...just a maggot."

Stephen leaned over and hugged Josh, spilling tears and snot on Josh's sweater. It felt like hugging a big toy bear. He tried to speak, but his pride stepped in.

If you only knew how much you mean to me...

"I'll take care of you, big bro."

The nickname pulled Stephen's thoughts toward a dim

light at the end of a dark tunnel.

He hasn't called me that since high school.

"For starters, let me handle the media fiasco."

"Oh, fuck no. This is the last thing I need, Josh."

Josh squeezed him tighter. "I know, big bro. I know." He let him go and straightened Stephen's shirt, ruffled his hair. "That's why I'm handling it."

I'm taking double my dose tonight. That sounds just perfect...

"I had no idea it got this big," Stephen said.

"Let me guess, you haven't been answering your phone either, have you?"

Stephen picked up the glass and downed what was left of the booze. He felt like he was in that nightmare again, pulled by the whim of the mighty ocean. Its freezing waters made him shiver.

I've always been the one there for Josh. The bullies, everything. Now he's the strong one. Oh, god, have I sunk this low?

"I don't want to sleep alone in the house tonight."

"Sure. Anything, bro. Like I said, I'm here." A tear welled in his eye and then trickled down his plump cheek. He laid his hand on Stephen's knee and shook it. "Whatever you need."

"Thanks."

Shelley's going to love this...

Stephen took his last drag off his cigarette and flicked it into the back yard. Pins and needles danced along his ethereal appendage. Memories of the wooden blocks scratched at the backs of his eyes like a caged rat.

HELP ME DADDY

Chapter 6

Stephen paused in Allie's doorway. Josh stopped behind him. He could still see the indentation her little body made on her small bed. For a moment, he smelled her lavender shampoo. Her toy cuckoo clock chimed. The little blue bird came out and chirped, pulling memories of Allie running through the house yelling "Cuckoo! Cuckoo!"

"You're scaring me, bro." Josh placed his hands on Stephen's shoulders and squeezed. A faint creak followed by a pop echoed through the small room. "I have no idea what we're doing here, man. *Why* are we in here?"

Stephen placed his hand on his brother's arm and felt goose bumps.

"I need to know that whatever I show you stays between us, okay?"

"Of course."

"Shelley, your wife, the goddamned mailman. It stays here, right?"

"Yeah, of course, big bro."

"I need you to be here for me, Josh. Okay?"

Josh laughed. "What have I been doing for a month? You're starting to really freak me out. Ouch! Let go. Stephen. You're *hurting* me."

"You promise first."

"I promise!"

Stephen released him, walked into Allie's room, and turned on the light. He took a deep breath, exhaled and closed his eyes.

Sure you wanna do this?

He opened his eyes and knelt down next to the blocks. They were jumbled, like when he found them the night before. They were like snakes, sunning themselves on the road, ready to strike his flesh, his sanity.

If I do this, it won't be the same. Nothing ever will...

Of all the thoughts bouncing around inside his head like bullets, the memory of him holding Allie for the first time when she was born entered and became an anchor of strength.

Help me, Bugga-boo. Help me be strong.

"I have to show you this, Josh."

The wood planks creaked in protest to Josh's girth as he trundled in.

"Show me what?"

Stephen closed his eyes again, took a deep breath, and thought of his little princess. He thought of his hands going through those golden locks as she slept atop him in their bed.

Do you pinky swear there are no monsters, Daddy?

He saw Allie's eyes sparkle when she unwrapped the dollhouse he made for her last Christmas.

Nothing is happening.

Thoughts raced through his mind while pinpricks became sparks, firing off and on, and up and down his phantom arm, as if it were asleep. Sweat ran down his forehead and collected on his chest. The flesh there began to itch, just like his arm.

"Just a little more..." Stephen reached out for the closest block. He heard his ethereal fingers slide across the dirty, hardwood floor toward the blue block with the letter H. "Just a little bit more."

Holy shit! I can feel the floor with my missing hand. Or is my mind...

"I don't like this, big bro. Whatever it is you want to talk about...let's talk. But this?"

Stephen slowly pushed the block a few inches across the floor. He let go of the worry, the memories, the pain, and almost collapsed. He wiped the sweat from his forehead, scooted back, and leaned against the wall. The world danced in front of his eyes as he tried to breathe.

I did it! I really made it move!

"What do you think?" Stephen said.

Josh stared down at the block that moved on its own. "You don't want to know."

The voice came from far away, and the dull thud became a pick-axe, boring deeper into Stephen's brain with each strike.

"Yes, yes I do, actually."

"I have to go before I regret saying something I shouldn't." Josh got up.

"Go? What? Josh!"

"We've *both* been under a lot of stress lately."

"You saw it. Just...just say it. You saw the block move."

"I saw fuckin' magic trick...I have to go now." Josh turned and walked down the hallway.

Stephen stood, feeling the euphoria ebbing and flowing.

"You can't go. I need you to be here for me like I was for you. Just please, tell me I'm not crazy.

"Look at you, Stephen! Is there something about you that I need to know, because you're really scaring me."

"There's nothing to be afraid of. Let's talk about it."

"Two days ago, Darlene asked me for a divorce. And when I asked her why, do you know what she said? She said that it's like *I'm* dead—I forgot *my* family."

"I'm sorry. I had no idea," Stephen managed as tiny streams clouded his vision. Air escaped his lungs. He leaned on the doorway, trying to breathe.

"You're not the only one suffering, okay? You want me

here night and day, I am. You want me to take you any-where, I will. You show me this...no more. Enough." Josh frowned. "Take a nice nap. And when you wake up, think about the lives of those who love you. The ones who are still *alive*." Josh stormed down the hallway and slammed the door behind him.

Stephen felt something rip in his chest like weathered canvas.

I'm losing it...

He walked toward the kitchen in search of a towel to clean himself up. On his way there, Stephen gently placed family portraits face-down as the canvas of his heart tore.

He balanced himself above the stove and wiped his mouth with the dishtowel. Minutes that felt like years passed as he paced around the house, thinking about his handgun and how painless it would be just to...

Outside, the storm picked up and bamboo smacked against the kitchen window.

The phone rang.

Stephen searched for the cordless and couldn't find it.

Hurry up or the answering machine will pick it up!

"Hello?"

"Hey."

Shelley's word, just one word, brought him back to the moment, centered him. The weight and anxiety faded away.

"I can't tell you how good it is to hear your voice," Stephen said.

"I'm sorry. I...I don't know what else to say," she said and her sobbing filled his mind. "I didn't mean to blow up on you."

"It's all my fault. I should have woken you up. I wasn't thinking straight. You have nothing to apologize for. Look, are you okay?"

If you still think I pushed you, we have a problem.

Right or wrong, we have a problem.

"Yeah, I'm okay." The sobbing grew until he felt it inside his stomach, churning what contents were left. "I'm just worried."

"About what?"

"Don't tell him I told you, but Josh called a few minutes ago. He said that you need to see a doctor. He said that something happened. I've never heard him sound so... *afraid.* Now I am, too. Please, tell me you're okay?"

Fibers within his chest knitted themselves back into the frail, sun-weathered canvas of his heart. For a moment, the bamboo smacking the kitchen window seemed greener, the world less gray.

"Shell, I can't go on without you."

"I...I want to come home if that's okay?"

"Yes!" The word came before he could stop it. He took a breath to control his excitement. "Yes, please come home."

"One condition."

Here we go...

"Name it."

"Promise me that you'll sit down with me so we can talk about your medication. I'm worried in more ways than one. You're slipping, and I don't know what I'll—"

I knew there was a catch. And now? Really?

"I promise."

Stephen heard a sigh, but he didn't know if it was relief, or something deeper, uglier.

"My parents will drop me off soon. They're not happy about this."

"I can imagine."

"I haven't even told them the half of it."

Aaaand here we have it! Do you send them pictures of my bowel movements too?

"I'll see you soon, then?"

"With this rain, about a half-hour."

"I love you, Shell."

A deafening silence was all Stephen could hear.

She still thinks I pushed her...

"Oh, one more thing," Shelley said.

"What's that?"

"I don't think we've paid the power bill. It's due today."

Stephen laughed for the first time in a thousand years. When Shelley joined in, that dim light at the end of that long, dark hallway became brighter. Emotions he hadn't felt since the accident welled up inside him, soothing him.

"I'll see you soon," Shelley said.

"Sounds good." Stephen turned the phone off and let out a deep sigh. He took in long, deep breaths, savoring the moment and the emotional chords she struck.

He giggled, feeling silly for turning the family pictures on their faces and walked over to them, correcting each one, wiping the dust off of Allie's picture. The hole in his heart widened, feasting on each fleeting moment of love the portraits produced and gave nothing in return but aches and grumbles for more.

"Josh, you fat, son-of-a-bitch, I love you." he grabbed the key to the mailbox, and headed outside, wondering how long it was since either of them actually checked the mail. Not to mention *bills*.

Chapter 7

Stephen closed the front door behind him and jiggled the keys to the mailbox in his hand.

How many bills do we have?

He yawned, eager to curl up in bed with Shelley.

Shelley, what would I do without you?

The air was crisp and cool. As he walked down the sidewalk, he watched the low boughs of the oak trees sway with the storm. Like the bamboo, they were greener, healthier than he remembered. Raindrops pelted Stephen's head, adding a strange, unique rhythm to the drums that still played inside.

FORECLOSED and SHORT SALE! signs dotted the neighborhood lawns.

Stephen stared up at the hole in the sky and the clouds that encircled it—their edges a molten pewter. Faster and faster they churned, when he heard *the* melody. The wind carried it like a contagion. It permeated him, slithering into every pore, its tendrils seeking his nerves.

A dull thud burrowed into his brain. An oil-slick tear dropped from the chaos above and landed on the street. White, blue and red moved and spilled into one another. A motor whined and *the ice cream truck* came to life.

It moved on tires that warped the road and reality beneath them. The sound echoed off the houses, squeezing his head.

A little girl ran out from his house.

"No...oh, *no*," Stephen said, and if his throat didn't close, he would have called her name. When his paralysis broke, he ran after her. *"Allie! Stop."*

One golden pigtail bounced up and down the left side of her head with every stride she took toward the truck.

Spots danced in front of his eyes as he raced after her.

The ice cream truck burned like a mirage in the desert.

"Ice cream man!" Little Allie bounced up and down beneath the service window.

"Allie, stop!" Stephen said, and when she did, his eyes fell upon a face as beautiful as it was horrific. Gray, milky eyes, once the color of the Caribbean Sea, stared back at him. The left one had popped and oozed its yellow contents across her cheek, like her tiger makeup he applied last Halloween.

And when you're old enough, you'll get to go scuba-diving with us, yeah?

A small spider crawled out of that socket and fretted about her face as a smile from cracked lips loosed streams that gave the rain puddles around her Scooby-Doo shoes a red hue.

Don't faint. Breathe!

"Allie, Baby, it's, me. It's Daddy." His tears added a salty twist to the rain. "Everything is okay now, Princess. I'm going to take you home now."

"Daddy?" Her smile twisted into a grimace. She turned toward the truck, looked into the open service window, and when Stephen saw where the other pig-tail used to be—where the metal severed her...

Why can't she see me?

"I need help! I lost my Mommy and Daddy!" Allie banged on the side of the truck. Her little, dirty fists, left dark smears.

"Well, howdy there, Lil' Miss. What kinda ice cream ya' want?" the man said around the block lodged in his throat. His voice sounded like an old guitar, missing a few strings.

It made Stephen's ears itch.

Am I invisible?

Darrell, the ice cream man, emerged from the service window and leered at Allie. Furnaces burned from where his eyes used to be. The tips of the flames distorted his face; reminiscent of Salvador Dali's melted clocks.

A cramp slithered through Stephen's bowels.

"I want my Mommy!"

"Oh, I'm sorry, little girl. Don't know if I can help with *that*."

Stephen ran to her and tried to grab her, only to feel his hand go through vapor.

"Oh, don't cry. I'm sure I've got somethin' for a little princess like you in here...someplace."

"Allie. Look at me!"

Use your other hand.

"Here you go." Darrell held out a waffle cone stuffed with little, pink severed tongues. They wiggled like maggots and spilled out. "I've got a little girl just like you. Likes to draw eyes on the little ones...so they can see. Wouldn't you like to *see*, little darlin'?"

Stephen reached out for Allie. Gravity pulled his hand toward Darrell. A cold, wet hand cinched around Stephen's wrist. Things slithered beneath that cold, soggy flesh, begging to be birthed.

Darrell faced him. Squiggles from a child's black crayon danced above spiraling galaxies swirling from dead sockets.

A small wooden block swelled his throat. A smirk loosed maggots hiding inside the cracks in his lips.

What air was left in Stephen's lungs escaped until his throat choked it off.

Stephen reached out and tried to grab little Allie-bear's wrist.

"It's Daddy, Baby. You have to run!"

Allie's face darkened as the rain intensified.

Thunder rolled above as Stephen watched reality blink out from the lightning.

Allie's head cocked to one side and she gasped.

"Daddy?"

"Run!"

Darkness fell upon them. Time slowed to a crawl. Below the melody of the ice cream truck, there was a song, barely audible above the tearing of his heart's fabric.

Allie's pigtail lifted and unwound. Frayed edges unraveling like a rope. Her whole body came apart in thin, confetti strips. They floated upward, lapped up by the abyss above. Before he let go of her hand, her fingers encircled his pinky as the last vestiges of her were absorbed into a crack in the sky.

"Let me go!" Stephen said.

Galaxies became bellows and flames flickered to life. Darrell smiled, exposing jagged ivory that glistened as he inhaled, as though he were savoring the moment.

A rain drop fell into Darrell's eye, extinguishing the flame. He winced, loosening his grip on Stephen.

What the fuck was that? Did that just hurt him?

Inside the empty socket, a new flame came to life, popping and crackling.

Darrell tightened his grip and Stephen screamed as he felt every electrical tendon strain to their limits. Stephen ground his teeth as he stood on tiptoes, trying to angle his body to avoid the pain.

"Stop!"

Darrell's smile split, exposing teeth that ran all the way down his throat.

"Listen up good, Hoss. You try to interfere again, I'll burn you and everyone and *everythin'* in your life. I'll start with that little princess of yours. Are we crystal?"

Stephen looked into those eyes and saw another world

where countless feet had tread across countless highways, where children danced in a circle, holding hands, eyes and mouths stitched shut.

Darrell pointed at a single black line on the side of the truck and traced it with his finger-tips.

"One down. Three to go."

Stephen watched the ice cream truck—and the darkness that still held sway—dissolve and float up into the sky, like Allie did. Before the rupture closed, he spied towers over myriad cities.

Somewhere, in the distance, Stephen heard a train's siren.

"Allie!" he managed and then fainted.

Chapter 8

"Stephen! Oh, dear God," Shelley said.

Rain drops splashed atop Stephen's jittery eyelids. A projector opened in his mind and he watched Allie's golden pig tail bounce mere inches from his fingertips.

I touched her shirt.

"I'm calling an ambulance," Shelley said, pulling her cell out of her pocket. "We're in the neighbor's yard for Christ's sake. What happened?"

"No! No ambulance. We have to get inside."

He rolled over in the puddle and hoisted himself up. A cool wind blew against his feverish face.

Shelley reached down and took his hand, pulling him up.

The world swam as little red dots tainted it.

Don't faint again. I have to show her.

"We have to get you to a hospital."

"After I show you what I showed Josh—you'll understand. There's nothing any doctor can do for me, or, well, *us*. We're in this together now, for Allie."

She gasped at the utterance of her daughter's name. Her hand covered her mouth.

"You've lost your mind, and here I am playing right along. I shouldn't have come back."

"After you see this, you can leave. But I doubt you'll want to. Just, please, humor me for once."

She closed her phone and pocketed it. "Show me. And when I'm done packing, I'll drop you off at the hospital. Look at you!"

Stephen took her hand, caressing the inside of the palm. He pulled her toward the front door, tightening his grip as they approached. "Follow me." Stephen opened the door and ran down the hallway, headed toward Allie's room.

Shelley let go of his hand.

Stephen paused in the doorway. "What?"

"I can't...I can't go in there. You know that. And when did you get the courage—"

"Can you at least just watch the blocks? Please?"

Shelley crossed her arms.

"Fine. But can we hurry up this whole *you losing your marbles*, and just get to the hospital, hell, the psychiatric ward would probably be best."

"You may need a psychiatric ward after seeing this."

Stephen entered Allie's bedroom and sat down next to the blocks.

"Watch." He closed his eyes and tried to erase his mind, making room for Allie-bear. A memory surfaced: The sun gleamed off her golden hair, and azure eyes squinted against a sun he hadn't seen in a month. Or was it two? Hard to tell these days. Allie peddled around him in a circle on her first bicycle, smiling.

Look at me, Daddy! I'm riding it, I'm riding it!

Heat coursed up and down his lost arm while its fingers twitched from a low current growing with every shock. Wet fingertips slid across the wooden floor to the closest block.

It hurts, Daddy! Why did you let me fall down?

Stephen heard the blocks squeak across the floor. He brushed the closest one and it moved a few inches.

A gasp came from behind.

Help me, Allie. Help me, please. Let's show Mommy you need help, because I can't do this alone, Bugga-boo.

A weight lifted and the current intensified. Stephen reached out with the last little bit of strength he had and lifted the block a few feet in the air.

"Whaaa..." Shelley moaned and walked into the room.

"Allyson, what do you need, Baby?" he asked, "Where are you, Allie-bear?"

He opened his eyes and watched Shelley. She waved her hand around the block he was putting in place and recoiled as if bitten.

MOMMY DADDY HELP

A pang ran up his spine as he watched all of the color fade from Shelley's face. She brought her hands to her mouth and fell to her knees in front of the blocks and began to sob. Stephen let go and went to her, embraced her.

"It's okay, Baby. It's okay. Breathe, Love, breathe."

A snot bubble burst from her nose and the flood works followed, leaving trails down her face. He stroked her hair and rocked her. Her small frame shook as she gasped for breath.

"Still think I'm crazy? Stephen's voice broke."

Shelley wiped her tears away and faced him. "I hear her crying. Every night, I hear her crying. Ever since..."

"Shhh, Baby. Calm down. Just breathe for me. Take it slow."

"One night, I *knew* she was in our room. It was like she was in the corner, all curled up. I got up and got her favorite blanket. But when I came back, I couldn't hear her anymore. I've been in her room before and—"

"I know, Baby. I know. It's okay."

"Is it possible? I mean...what are we going to do?"

"Whatever it takes. That's what we do. Whatever it takes. We need help, though. I'll call Josh over for dinner tonight. We'll put our brains together, because we don't have much time, Shell."

"Where is she, Stephen? *Where?*"

"Trapped. Somewhere she's not supposed to be, with *him*."

Chapter 9

"Pass the potatoes, please." Josh's sausage sized fingers twitched in anticipation. "Thank you. It's so good to see you two together again. Shelley, you look amazing."

"Josh, I wouldn't—" Shelley said.

"I misspoke," his tongue tried to say around the mashed-potatoes. "What I meant to say is—I don't know—there's just a really good vibe around you guys." He shoved another mouthful in. "Had a chance to call the doctor and schedule an appointment yet?"

"Yeah. I called his office this afternoon," Stephen said "I told them it was important, and he actually called me back."

"Really?"

"Yeah." Stephen motioned for Josh to pass him the potatoes.

Josh passed the bowl to Stephen.

"Thanks. I told him about the pain. He says it's normal and to not worry about it. But in the event things don't subside in a few months, or—God forbid, it gets worse—he wants to see me as soon as possible."

"Good, good. I'm really glad to hear that. You really had me freaked out for a while there. What did he have to say about the blocks?"

Shelley coughed, almost choking on her food.

"I didn't tell him."

"You didn't?"

"What have *you* seen?" Shelley asked. A low-flame

flickered just behind her hazel eyes.

Dough-Boy's face turned as red as summer lobsters. His mouth flapped open and closed.

"I showed Shelley once she got home. This time, I did a bit more than just move a block."

"We talked, well, *communicated* with Allie," Shelley said.

Josh stopped chewing and brought his napkin to his lips. He formed a pudgy steeple with his hands.

"I think it's time we talk about it," Shelley said.

Josh fidgeted in his seat and played with his napkin.

"The kids woke me up at like...two in the morning, talking about a little girl rummaging through their toys."

The hairs on the back of Stephen's neck rose.

I knew it!

Shelley poured a round of drinks. She downed hers.

"Annie says she sees a little girl with one pigtail come around every now and then. When it storms really bad, especially. I also found Susan talking to no one in her room once."

"Was it Allie?" Stephen said, motioning with his hand to hurry it up. "Was it?"

Josh bit down hard on his fist. "Hell, I'm not a psychic!"

Stephen looked at Shelley, and for a moment, it was like they shared the same mind.

"I think that's exactly what we need, Josh," Stephen said.

"What? You want me to find a psychic? A paranormal specialist?"

Stephen pushed his empty plate away. "Perhaps we'll need a demonologist. This...Darrell, he's not going to stop. I think he's just begun. He's toying with me, *us*."

Josh took a deep breath and pushed his plate forward.

That's the first time I've seen him not be able to finish his plate.

"I might be a P.I., but I don't know anyone who knows anything about the paranormal... "

"You must know someone"

Pull your head out of your hippy-haze and think, you fat bastard!

"Oh wait..." Josh said. "A year ago, I had a client, old man. Hired me to watch his daughter. He thought she was dealing drugs. Well, when I gave him the proof, he told me that he already knew it."

"And?" Stephen said.

"He said he just needed the pictures to show the police. And when he sees me looking at him the way I did, he told me what I had for dinner, how our mother died of cancer, when my daughter would break her leg! To the day!"

"When can you call him?" Shelley said.

"I...it's too late now. I'll call him tomorrow."

"Tomorrow is too late, Josh. Let's get serious here."

Josh held his hands up in surrender. "Okay, okay. I'll call him. But my client list is at home. When I get home I'll give him a call. Okay?"

Stephen looked over at Shelley and they both nodded.

"Right, well, the sooner you get home, the better," Shelley said rising from her seat.

"Oh! And the news report said that Darrell's wife is missing. Maybe he can, I don't know, tap into her?"

"She's dead."

"What?" Stephen said, meeting Shelley's gaze. "When?"

"I've been doing a little digging, okay? I got the call from, well, a friend on the police force. They identified her body a few hours ago. I wasn't going to say anything, because... we've all been under stress, right?"

"Go on..." Stephen said.

Josh let out a big sigh. He ran a hand over his balding head. "They found his "missing" wife, man. She's dead. Right where the accident happened. They also found another one of those blocks shoved down her throat."

"Get home and call the psychic. Call us as soon as you can," Stephen said. "We need to know, why us? Why Allie? Oh..." he scratched his chin, "it may be nothing, but ask him about water."

"Water?" Josh said.

"When I confronted Darrell, a raindrop landed in his eye—they're both like, mini volcanoes. Well, it put the fire out."

"Confront Darrell? What? When?"

"Yesterday, before Shelley got back. I went to check the mail and... the ice cream truck fell from the sky. Allie ran to him...

Shelley squeezed his hand under the table. Her face looked like it could crack.

"You...you think water can hurt him?" Josh asked.

Stephen took the shot glass from Shelley and finished it. "It came back as soon as it went out. But...just ask the psychic about it. It could be important. We don't have much to go on here."

"We're not sleeping until we hear from you," Shelley said and squeezed Stephen's hand harder.

"Well, I guess I should get my fat ass in gear," Josh said as he stood.

Stephen got up from the table, walked over to Josh and embraced him. "Don't take your eyes off your kids. Darrell warned me there would be more. Promise me you won't take your eyes off them, okay?"

"I promise." Josh patted him on the back.

Shelley joined in the embrace.

Chapter 10

"Why the fuck hasn't Josh called yet? It's almost midnight," Stephen said, pacing back and forth over black and white kitchen tiles. He stared at them wondering how simple his life would be if, it too, were just black and white.

"Try calling him again," Shelley said. She entered the kitchen holding Allie's Nerf water gun. She cocked it and her eyebrow as well. "Whaddya' think?"

"I don't understand."

Shelley placed it atop the counter and took his hand. Despite the sweatiness of her palm, it still felt nice.

"What are you going to do with *that?*"

"You said that when you saw him, Darrell, that a raindrop put out the flame in his eye."

"Yeah, it did...for a little while."

"Well, it's something, right? I mean, if he comes after us..."

Stephen hugged her, inhaled the rain-fresh scent of her hair. "You're a genius, Shell. I knew there was a reason I married you."

Shelley pinched the nape of his neck. "Try calling him again." She opened the top of Allie's water gun, walked over to the sink and pulled the lever to the faucet.

"He keeps sending me to voicemail. He's probably sitting back and smoking his fuckin' hookah."

"If he doesn't answer we should just go over there."

"I've always had to put my foot up his ass to get him to do anything."

Shelley finished filling the water gun and turned off the faucet.

"Save it for helping Allie."

She placed a hand on Stephen's shoulder.

"Pick up, pick up, pick up, pick up..."

"I'm driving," Shelley said, grabbing the keys.

"And I'm going to kill him."

~

They pulled up in Josh's driveway. All the lights were off, but his car was there.

Stephen ran his fingers through his hair and cinched down, pulling a few out. The pain centered him. "Let's go."

He got out of the passenger's seat and closed the door behind him, expecting a light, any light, to turn on inside the house.

Didn't expect us coming over, did you?

Shelley's door slammed, and when she joined him, she reached out and grabbed his hand.

In the rain, they sprinted to the front door.

Stephen pushed the doorbell and didn't let go.

Shelley pounded on the door with her fists.

Nothing.

"I can't believe this, Shell. What the fuck is he doing?"

"Look!" She pointed to the kitchen window. "The light just came on."

Stephen pounded on the door until it opened. All he could see was darkness.

"Hey, big bro. Hey, Shell. Come on in."

Stephen stepped inside with Shelley behind him. It smelled worse than anything he'd ever smelled before; a mixture of iron and dead skunks.

"Josh?" Stephen said, fumbling for a light switch. He found it and flipped it on.

Nothing.

"Josh?" Shelley said, bumping into Stephen. "Where are you, and why is it so dark?"

"Do you smell that?" Stephen whispered.

"Yeah, what the hell is that? Roadkill?"

"I'm back here in my office, guys."

Stephen searched his pockets for his lighter, but couldn't find it. Instead, he used his hands to find the walls and stumbled to the doorway. Shelley bumped into him again.

"Why haven't you answered my calls, Dough-boy? It's only been a few hours. Did you get so high you found the fifth dimension, and made friends with Tinkie-Winkie?"

Josh laughed heartily. "Something like that."

"Come on, enough. Turn the lights on," Stephen said.

"Wish I could, man. But when I called the psychic—"

"You called the psychic?"

"Can I finish?"

Stephen and Shelley exhaled in unison.

"Thank you. You guys need to understand I'm only doing what the psychic told me to do..."

The light flashed on.

Josh sat in his chair in front of his desk with his handgun pointed at the side of his head. The sweater and khaki pants he wore at dinner were stained with blood.

The room spun.

The warm, wet muscle in Stephen's chest raced. "Josh, put the gun down, *now!*"

"I'm only doing what the psychic told me to, big bro." Josh let out another laugh.

Shelley moved beside Stephen.

Maybe, just maybe, I can move closer and take the gun away. If I'm quick enough...

"The psychic told me we can deal with this the hard way or the easy way. I'm choosing the easy way, man. That's what's up!"

The gun's barrel left the side of his head, and for a brief moment, Stephen could have sworn he saw a shadow standing behind Josh.

"You're not gonna give up, Josh. We're here for you. Aren't we Shelley?"

"Think about the kids, Josh."

"I did, Shelley, I did. It was the biggest mistake I ever made."

"Let...let me talk to the psychic, okay?" Stephen said.

"You can't talk to a dead man."

"But you said you talked to him." Shelley's grip became painful, which Stephen welcomed.

"I did. And as soon as I said, I need some answers, I heard a gunshot."

Stephen took a step back while he watched Josh's face lose its color. It began to shift, distort. Black crayon squiggles appeared above his eyes.

Furnaces replaced them.

"You ain't got the common sense to wad a shotgun, Hoss." Josh's voice changed as he was hijacked. A deep, discordant, southern drawl seeped in. "Which is fine by me."

Glistening rows of jagged ivory pushed out his teeth, replacing them. The old ones clattered on the floor like Tic Tacs. They split the sides of his mouth, forging rows down his throat, rending bone, muscle and sinew. The fat in his cheeks leaked out and hit the floor in three loud plops.

Stephen didn't wince when Shelley screamed, or when her nails pierced the flesh of his palm.

"Stephen," Shelley said, her voice distant, underwater, as she backed away, "we need to leave, now!"

Show Shelley you're not your father.

"Not without answers first. What are you doing with my daughter?"

"You want answers, that right, Stevie?"

Darrell scratched the side of his head with the handgun, "last man tried to figure that one out got a bullet in his head. Lard-ass here ain't got no sense, neither. Started rattlin' on to his wife, his kids. So, I blew their brains out. Sorry about the smell."

Why do I have the feeling this is a trap?

"I'm just trying to figure out what you want, Darrell. So, let's put the gun down, and I'm sure we can talk this out."

Darrell's laugh reminded Stephen of gravel crunching.

Oh, we'll get our answers. Bet on it, you twisted fuck...

"Here's ya' answers: Kill yourself. It's that simple, Stevie. If you do, my daughter gets a play-mate. She's been so lonely." Darrell swayed in the chair pointing the gun at Stephen.. "You? That's answer territory, ain't it? Look, I'll spare ya' brother. Like my Daddy always said: Fair is fair."

"Why am I so goddamned important?"

Darrell brought the barrel of the gun back to the side of Josh's head and thumbed back the hammer.

"Oh...and you were gettin' so close. Keep bein' ornery, see where that gets ya.'"

"Why do you want me to kill myself?"

"Reckon you wouldn't come out of the rain if it were a hailstorm. If you don't kill ya'self, then goodbye Lard-ass! *And* that pretty wife of yours."

Anger welled up in Stephen like an air-bag inflating after a crash.

"If I do what you want..."

"Go on, Hoss. It's your dime."

"...what do I get in return?"

Darrell pursed his lips and cocked his head. "Sounds like another *answer* question. Nope. Last chance, fancy-pants. Either Jabba here, and that pretty little thang goes, or you go. Best you'd think this through."

"Shelley!"

Darrell sighed, the bellows in his eyes grew and began

to spin. The anger wafting off his brother's hijacked body.

That's the key. Why does he want me to kill myself? What does that give him?

"Now, I'm bein' real nice here. I'll give ya' one last shot, Hoss. We can do this the hard way, or the easy way. Call it."

Stephen felt Shelley bump into him. Out of the corner of his eye, he saw the barrel of Allie's water gun.

Darrell cocked his head, squinted his eyes. "The hell is that for? Have you lost ya' mind?"

Shelley moved in front of Stephen and leveled the barrel at Darrell's face. "You like taking people's children?"

She pulled and held the trigger down, spraying Darrell's face. The stream hit both eyes. Smoke drifted out from the dead sockets as the fires died. The smell reminded Stephen of camping.

Darrell began to chuckle. "Close, but no cigar. Not here, no, sir. Rules don't work that way."

Orange glowed deep within Darrell's eye sockets, spinning, until they turned red. Flames shot out a few feet, singing Stephen's shirt.

Shelley leaped back and cocked the water gun again.

"These flames are lit by a hate, so deep, it's eternal, Hoss. *Death* couldn't take it! You think a kid's toy gun will?"

"Fuck you!" Shelley said.

Darrell's face vanished and Josh's returned.

The gun went off.

Stephen tried to close his eyes but could only squint. Wet brain matter hit the wall and reminded him of the rotten pumpkins he and his friends used to smash on the streets after Halloween.

He felt dizzy, like he was underwater again.

Memories fell from his mind like leaves in November... the smell of the summer grass the jocks had made Josh eat like a goat...until Stephen arrived, just in time. The look of fear on Josh's face when Stephen set him up with Darlene back in high school. How Josh had held him—being the bigger brother for once—when Mom had exhaled her last breath. The hulk of a man he had latched onto as he walked into her room with that smell of dead roses and mold. Eyes that saw red with every heartbeat watched the world swim in front of him.

"Stephen!" Shelley called from the front door.

Stephen tried to breathe, to think, but the world was spinning too fast for eyes that didn't want to see it anyway. He stood, paralyzed, waiting for the gun to level on him.

If he wants me dead, why doesn't he kill me?

Shelley grabbed Stephen's arm and pulled.

His paralysis broke. He followed her out as he watched his dead brother slide down from his chair to the floor.

They ran outside, into the rain. Shelley pulled out her keys and hit the button to unlock the doors.

"Stephen! Let's go. *Now!*"

An ice cream truck appeared on the road, in front of Josh's driveway. A horn blared.

Darrell opened the service window, bellowing laughter his cheeks split from the strain.smiled, waving. He marked four more lines next to the others, honked the horn again, and drove off.

Chapter 11

A lifetime of memories blew through Stephen's mind like the storm as it tore the dead leaves from the trees looming over the back porch. Lightning struck, illuminating the debris as it danced. The last words his mother spoke before she passed haunted him: *Take care of each other. Especially Josh. He needs it.*

"Do you want another drink?" Shelley said.

"No. I'm good."

"Talk to me, Stephen. We have to focus on—"

"Darrell's been using me. He's been using me to do...oh God..." Stephen leaned over and Shelley embraced him. She rocked him back and forth.

"It's like I'm his keystone. I can't go on like this, Shell."

"I have no idea what it's like to lose a brother. I guess I'm lucky...being an only child." Shelley moved closer to him and rubbed his back. "But know that I'm here for you." A quirky smile erupted on her beautiful face. "No matter what."

"I think I know why I'm so important to him. I think I know how to trick him. But," Stephen's body tensed as his pills in their little plastic bottles called out to him. "I can't do it. I'll fuck it up."

"Wha...what do you mean?"

"Everything I've wanted I've fucked up. I'm just like my father."

"Don't say that, Love. You know that's not true. You— we— stood up to Darrell!"

"When I was three years old, my father tried to leave us. My mother said I followed him around the house, running, screaming, begging him *not* to leave. He stayed. But when we found out Mom had cancer...he left."

"I thought you said your father—"

"Yeah, I lied to hide how dysfunctional the family was. He was a monster, in every sense of the word."

"What did he do?"

"I came home one day after school. It must have been early afternoon. They were fighting. I followed the trail of broken latticework, overturned potted flowers, and shattered picture frames inside. I saw him punch her. And it was *hard*. My mother, probably in stage-two cancer, had they caught it by then...I watched her blood fly and splatter the tile floor. He turned and saw me. And when he did, I saw, I saw someone, *something* different. But as he kept beating her...for the life of me, I couldn't stop him. I couldn't stop him. Not then. I don't think I can save her, Shell."

Shelley cuddled up next to him and stroked his black locks. "What did you see in him?"

"The same thing I see in the mirror. I remember the day I flushed his pills down the toilet. He broke my arm that day."

Shelley winced.

"He was a pill-head. And look at what I've become."

"Stop! You're not your father. Stop beating yourself up."

He stared at her face, a face with strength, and for the first time, he was jealous of her. Stephen felt electricity course from the nub of his shoulder down ethereal pathways. "No, it's worse."

"What do you mean?"

"I saw our daughter. I saw her. Her face—what she became. And this," he held up a phantom arm, "how long before I kill you, or me? Every *fucking* day it gets worse, *heavier*. More people are dying....Josh called Darrell a terrorist once...he's *far* worse."

Shelley blinked and tears spilled from red eyes. "I believe in you. I wouldn't be here if I didn't. I love you, Stephen."

"I love you too."

"This is our daughter we're talking about." Shelley drew in a breath. "I need you to be strong. Can you?"

"I have an idea." He pulled a cigarette out of its pack and lit it. A slow burn rippled his lungs. "If he wants me dead so bad, then why hasn't he killed me? And, more importantly, why am I so important to him dead?"

"I don't know."

"We'll trick him. He wants me dead and he wants me there, with him."

"How do we trick him?"

"That's where you come in. I'm going to need your help—Allie's going to need your help."

"Sure. Anything."

"You, my love, are going to the hospital to get some supplies. You can still do that, right?"

"Depends on the supplies. What are you talking about?"

"You've had to induce comas in patients, right?"

"More times than I can count."

"And you know how to bring them out, right?"

"Yeah—Whoa, whoa, stop right there. Just what are you talking about?"

"You put me out, as far out as you can, and we go from there."

"I think you're out of your mind." Shelley stood and walked toward the French doors. She opened them and looked upon the gloom outside. "I'm not helping you kill yourself."

"I'm not asking that! Just put me out, and if worse comes to worst, you can always pull me out."

"You haven't thought this through. You run the risk of killing yourself. No, we're going back to the drawing board with this one. Have you even thought about *me*?"

"Do you have a better idea? I *refuse* to wake up one more day, shaking, scared—knowing where our daughter is."

"You're actually serious about this?"

"*I'm* not. *We* are. Anything it takes."

He took his last drag and flicked the butt into the back-yard while Shelley stared at him, studying him.

"And what if you're wrong? What if Darrell kills you?"

"I don't know. All I do know is that time is running out. It's almost like she's deeper...distant. And what my arm did...I have a feeling that has a lot to do with it, too. We don't have any other choices, Love. We have to play in his playground. And if I'm not dead, just in a coma, he'll never see it coming."

"I can't believe I'm considering this. If I get caught, which—there is a huge chance I will—I'm in jail."

"You won't get caught."

"Oh, I just walk into the hospital and steal whatever I want?"

"Pretty much."

"You're kidding me."

"Shelley, my love, I have all the faith in the world in you."

"I'm glad someone does."

Stephen went to Shelley and wiped the tears from her face. Her amber hair smelled like vanilla. He lost himself in her scent and the way the light seemed to pool and swirl within her. He fell in love with her all over again.

"Oh God, what are we about to do?"

"We're going to save, Allyson."

Chapter 12

"Are you ready?" Shelley held the bag out to him like he was a homeless man asking for a handout.

"What do I do?"

She sat in front of him and pulled bottles and a syringe from the bag. Shelley held the containers up to him. "I inject you with this and you go out. This *can't* fail!"

Stephen reached out with his hand and cupped her face, bringing it up to his level.

"I love her more than life itself."

"We both do."

Stephen held a tingling, ethereal appendage up in the air and was amazed to see a faint blue shimmer around an arm that looked exactly like the one he had before the wreck.

Why can't Shelley see it?

"Here, he can do whatever he wants. I want to see what it's like when I go there. You saw how he reacted to the water. He said...something about rules. But there? Besides, that's where the rain is coming from. *There*." He pointed at the sky.

"What if we're wrong? This is too big of a risk. I can't do this. No, I refuse." Shelley started putting the contents back into the bag.

"Even if I am wrong, she won't be alone. Even if I die, I'll be there for her."

Shelley ground her teeth.

God I hate it when she does that...

"So you *are* being selfish. Your father would be so proud of you right now."

Her words seared him like a cigarette burn: slow at first, and by the time realization sunk in, nerves were dead and the flesh that housed them charred.

Shelley stood and headed for the hallway, carrying the bag with her.

"Without me, or you, she's out there, Shell... She's by herself with that...that *thing*. If given the chance, wouldn't you sacrifice yourself?"

"You're not coming back are you?"

"That depends on you, Love. Give me five minutes. Then bring me back. No matter what, I don't want to lose you, but I can't go on living knowing where Allie is." He looked into her eyes. "*We* don't have a choice."

Shelley walked back into the room, sat the bag on the table, and gathered a legal pad and a pen. She set them by Stephen's ethereal arm, and placed Allie's water gun beside them. She steeled him with her gaze. "Don't break contact. If you do, I'll bring you back."

Shelley stuck the needle in one of the see-through bottles and pulled back on the plunger.

"Let me see your arm."

He held it out to her and she wrapped a tube around his arm above his elbow and pulled. For a moment, it felt tingly like his ethereal arm. She rested the tip of the needle on the biggest vein and took a deep breath.

"Let's save her, Stephen. Let's save our baby."

She bent down and kissed his lips until he felt her warm tears splash on his cheek.

"I love you, Shell."

"I love you too."

"Shoot me up. Put me out. Before I lose my nerve."

"If you can't make it, if something happens...tell her I love her. Tell her that her mommy misses her very, very much."

Stephen caressed her face and brought it to his.

"Be strong for us, Baby. Be strong for Allie."

She nodded and brought the needle to his arm. "Here we go."

Chapter 13

Stephen floated with sparkling dust motes surrounding him. He felt like he was on a roller coaster climbing up the steep track before the deep plunge. He saw Shelley sitting over his body. He reached out for her, fingertips only feet away, but a force continued to pull him upward. It carried on it a chorus of voices singing a perverted melody.

The living room grew darker, hazier. As he rose higher, the boards in the attic and the tiles on the roof moved through him without effort.

Where are you, Baby?

Globs of pearlescent dew pelted him from the churning maelstrom just beyond the inkblot of cracked sky. Steel wool clouds parted to reveal a desiccated landscape. Barely visible, a train straddled silvery webs, spilling a piss-yellow glow from its windows: The Lost Ones with their chorus like countless bees trapped inside empty soda cans filled his head. Like a lamp through fog, beach-blonde hair glowed from the center.

I'm coming, Allie.

Stephen reached up and saw the arm he had lost shimmering blue. He wiggled his fingers and felt the pen in his hand. He wrote as best as he could: *I love you.* Stephen reached for Allie's water gun and felt his fingers pass right through it.

We were wrong...fuck!

He began to unravel like ribbons; like Allie-bear did. Euphoria flooded him as his body was deconstructed until memory itself...

Chapter 14

...came back as he entered the midnight of this other world. Stephen gasped, taking in the hot, putrid air that burned his eyes and seared his lungs until they refused any more abuse. He flopped like a fish on the end of a spear on the slippery cobblestones. He touched his face with his healthy arm.

Good. Nice and solid. But the rain. Where's the rain?

Coughing, he brought up wet slurry from his chest.

Small, gray tendrils of mist drifted from the vast forest beyond the stones. The scent reminded him of a beach where dead fish had washed ashore. The massive trees swayed in the breeze, ablaze with shimmering demented versions of color no rainbow could produce. In the sky, a shattered moon drawn with a yellow crayon twitched back and forth as if it were controlled by strings.

He scrambled up the cobblestone walk, taking in short breaths and ran toward the iridescent forest, toward the hypnotizing song from the countless Lost Ones.

His shoes slid across smooth stones. The stones hid a thick, ankle-high river. Stephen tried to stop and almost fell backward. He came down on his hands and knees, as if he were bowing to whatever swirled in the darkness.

A pool of large, green algae spun around and slowly drained through the crack, dripping down to the real world below. The warm, viscous river moved over his legs and hands.

Where's the pen?

He walked over to the crack and looked down. He saw his home and the others that flanked it, as if they were underwater. He flexed his fingers and felt a familiar object. He made a circle with it first, just in case, and wrote: *I'm in.* He felt Shelley's warm hand touch his. He walked around the maw, feeling its pull, and entered the woods.

Stephen tried calling Allie's name and brought up more of what was steadily coating his once pink lungs. He reached out to a tree for support. His arm went inside it. His head smacked against the bark.

Pulling his arm free, he stumbled on. The voices he'd heard in dreams grew louder, like an old gospel record that was warped and skipped when you played it. In the distance, he could see the tip of a great pyre.

Above the smell of decay and rotten fruit, the scent of smoke tickled the hairs in his nostrils, and what it cooked made his stomach grumble. It reminded him of freshly cooked veal, medium rare.

"Allie." He managed, barely above a whisper. "Allie!"

The last call felt like puking razors. He pulled his shirt off and brought it to his face, breathing through the sweat and tears. A hum drifted above winds which snapped branches from trees that looked like they were drawn by children.

As soon as the gale came, it left, daring him to take another step. Something big thundered in the distance as it stepped, felling the massive trees. It didn't sound like normal trees; more like the fake Papier-mâché ones used in elementary school plays.

"Allie!" A cough followed.

Pull out! You're going to die.

Removing the shirt from his face, he hacked precious crimson across a distorted tree's root. Its roots sucked it up like it was drinking a milkshake with a straw. The sound poked at his eardrums. It creaked and groaned, and he felt the ground move underneath him.

Just write it: Pull me out!

"Where are you, Baby?"

Stephen brought the wet shirt to his face again. His stomach growled at the metallic aroma.

He heard something shamble close by. Dead leaves crunched under each step.

What the hell is it? I can't see shit.

He dropped to his knees and tried to hide the electric-blue his armed radiated by wrapping his shirt around it. Still, it illuminated the forest floor and the odd shapes that scurried over dead, wet leaves with neon-green veins. The wind picked up again and bent the trees. A branch scraped Stephen's cheek. He closed his eyes and fought the urge to cough.

Something grabbed his shoulder and squeezed.

"Stephen?" The voice was familiar, masculine, but distant.

Get out! Write Shelley now!

He wiggled his fingers and felt the pen. The smooth ball spilled ink across a page for his love to see...and stopped.

"Is that you, Stephen?"

Stephen took a deep breath. Whatever loomed over him, cast a shadow darker than the night.

Debris fell on Stephen's face, and when he looked into his lap, he saw yellow, fat maggots squirming. A few tore through his jeans and bit into him.

The thing leaned down and sat next to him.

"Josh?" Stephen managed.

That's not Josh. That's not my Dough-boy.

Josh opened his mouth and formed words over the creatures that spilled forth. Josh licked his lips and crunched down on the small river of deformed insects, chewing them up like granola. When Josh bit down on one, its goo landed on Stephen's cheek, burning, searing.

Stephen unwrapped his shirt from his arm and wiped it away.

"It's so good to see you, big bro. You finally offed yourself!"

"No, I...I'm here. I'm alive. I'm here for Allie." His chest, fighting for breath, filtered air through the bloodied shirt.

Josh's yellow eyes grew as round as the deformed moon above them.

"You have no idea what you've done. Wow, you've really fucked up this time. *He's here.*" Josh whispered the words, but the trees amplified the syllables, as if instructed to do so. "He was right... He was right." Josh let out a nervous laugh and almost choked on the flood of tiny beasts spewing from his mouth.

"What do you mean?"

"Look!" Josh pointed upward. "Do you see that?"

Stephen squinted. "See what? I don't understand."

"There, just beyond that star—that little glimmering orb. It's another one."

"Another what?"

"Do you think this is the only place like this? They're everywhere."

"What are you getting at?"

Josh pointed to a hill, just below the tip of a fire with embers that tickled the night air as they rose.

"That's where the old train derailed. Well, it's back...it's been back. And now you're here.

"Why? You're not making any sense."

Josh smiled, his jowls cracked all the way up to his ears. Centipedes scurried up his face and opened his lower eyelid, sliding inside. His cheek bowed from the bug tumbling about in his flesh.

"Why? Why not? These places are special, bro. You can do—be anything you want here. And he's got plans, my friend. Where we're going..."

"Allie...where is she? Does *he* have her?"

Josh laughed and helped Stephen up. Hundreds of things stretched his skin, giving birth.

"You still don't get it, do you?" he said.

Stephen could only stare.

"When he blew my brains out, I thought it was game over, man. But, I found them..." Josh motioned with his arm. Three sets of yellow eyes appeared behind Josh. Two sets were low, the one high. Their bodies were barely visible; shaking shadows that squiggled, like old celluloid caught in a reel, skipping.

Darlene and oh no... the kids.

Stephen's heart misfired. He made a fist and bit down. "Josh, have you seen Allie?"

"There's something about this place. Something magical. If you would just kill yourself, you'd understand. Just let go, man."

"Allie! Where is she? I'm taking her home."

"You think he's going to *let* you take her? As long as she's been here, I don't know. It's almost like it accelerated his plans. Well, that and his daughter has a new friend."

"Darrell...what has he done to her? What?"

Josh planted a blue, fat finger across his wreck of a mouth where grub worms gnawed away at what was left of his gums. Teeth plunked on the soft earth. "Shhhh! You don't say his name here."

Another gale shook the trees and snapped the smaller ones like toothpicks. From the distance, a shriek pierced Stephen's eardrums and brought the jackhammer inside his head to life. *Thud, thud. Thud, thud.*

"Help me, Josh. Where is she? Please...I don't have much time," he said, coughing up more life-juice.

Carrion on the ground came to life and lapped the fluid up like they were taking a drink from a river. Each one was drawn with a child's crayon, fuzzy, and out of proportion.

They jerked their limbs, snapping and popping, as they feasted while their gut-bags plopped on the ground. What used to be a small Jack Russell Terrier met Stephen's gaze. It growled.

Josh's eyes grew dimmer and began to fade into the darkness that enveloped them. More abominations ate away what was left of his face. Stephen closed his eyes and rubbed them, making a promise to remember Josh the way he was.

I'm here for Allie. Focus.

"Help me." Stephen repeated.

"I wish I could."

Stephen grabbed Josh's massive shoulders and shook. "I'm not giving you a choice!"

"It's too late for her. Don't you see that? I'm so, sorry, bro. Kill yourself and jump on board. If you don't," Josh lifted his arms and turned in a circle, "all of it...everything... ashes."

"Josh and his family swayed in the breeze. Minutes that felt like hours passed, until the familiar hum came again. It was a woman's voice. It reminded him of an old song he couldn't quite place.

"Where is she?

Josh pointed toward the source of the din and whispered: "Where else would she be? Where everyone goes, eventually. She's at the center of *them*. The ones who are too damaged."

The Lost Ones' shadows danced around a campfire. "She's scared. But not as much as you should be, big bro."

Josh closed the distance between them, cupped a soggy hand that smelled worse than a dead calf rotting in the hot sun, and whispered: "Follow the hum, bro. That's the one place he *can't* go."

Josh turned, disappearing into the primordial woods with the hazy shadows of what his family had become.

The gale above Stephen spun faster, whining like an old engine about to throw a piston. Detritus from the forest's floor spun up and circled him like little tornados, their gravity pulling him back, away.

Stephen heard the hum again; closer, crisper. He followed it, tripping over deadfall.

Something flew above him, casting yet another shadow darker than the night.

When it shrieked, Stephen covered his ear with one hand, while the other suffered what sounded like a dying cat. When it passed, he moved on.

Stephen broke into another coughing fit and had to stop. He brought the shirt up to his mouth, only to see tiny creatures with glowing red eyes on stalks staring back at him. He wretched, spilling whatever was in his stomach, as well as more precious blood.

I don't have much longer.

Shelley's voice spoke inside his mind: "Save our daughter, Baby. Save her."

His blue, shimmering hand reached into another world for the pen. When he found it, he wrote: *Time?*

Shelley's fingers touched his electric hand.

Five minutes. Good.

Stephen placed his shirt over his nose again. Out of the corner of his eye, he saw a dome that flickered like an oil spill in the summer. The hum transformed into a beautiful, haunting voice:

My Sarah lies over the ocean.

My Sarah lies over the sea.

My Sarah lies over the ocean.

Oh, please, bring back my Sarah to me.

Chapter 15

Stephen approached the small dome and stopped, taking it in. He could hear singing, but the dome muffled the sound.

What did you hide in here, Darrell?

Behind him, a tree fell.

A large Rottweiler with a depression in his sides from where a car had run him over shook on mangled legs.

"Oh...what sweet hell is this?" Stephen whispered.

A low, guttural growl escaped an ever-expanding mouth.

Stephen backed up, staring at its pregnant stomach.

No...anything but this...

Like wish-bones cracking, the Rottweiler's jaws split. It heaved like a cat with a hair-ball. Bone and sinew creaked and snapped as two tentacles whipped out of its mouth. They latched on to the sides of the dog's head, using it as leverage to give birth.

The mewling beast splashed on the ground. A pink mass bathed in crimson glistened under the perverted moonlight. Its tentacles flailed around countless frog-like heads. Their teeth chattered like a wind-up toy.

It rolled forward.

Stephen took another step back and felt something move through him. He reached out and touched the inside of the dome.

The beast threw itself at him, but collided with the protective shell. It slid down, leaving a trail of blood and organs.

He exhaled and took a deep breath of crisp, clean air.

The singing stopped.

Stephen turned.

Light spilled across a field of grass and onto a defunct trailer. The paint, long gone, was replaced with what looked like Bondo and moss. A shadow moved inside. A drawer, or maybe a cupboard opened. Silverware clanked.

He walked up to the mold covered steps and peeked in, but strings of beads obscured his vision. A little table with broken, wooden chairs surrounding it was all he could make out.

The strings of beads split and a woman rushed out, swinging a large knife.

"Darrell, I will cut you, and gut you like a fish, ya' hear?"

Stephen pin-wheeled back on his heels, but stopped just short of the protective dome and the gathering creatures outside it.

"I'm not Darrell! My name is Stephen Morrison," he said, holding up his arm in surrender.

Her gaze fixed on his neon-blue arm. Her mouth opened, and she dropped the knife.

"My...that's so pretty."

"Ummm...thanks," he said, still holding his arms up, "I'm here for my daughter."

"How'd you?" she scratched her head, "How'd you get in here? That ice cream truck bring ya'?"

"No, I...I had to do something else to come here."

"Know how long it's been since I had comp'ny?"

As she came closer, he could make out her features. Despite the purple bruises on her face and arms, she was beautiful. The once white dress she wore was faded, tattered. She looked like a prostitute after telling her pimp it had been a slow night. Except for the block that swelled her throat.

I found her!

"No, Ma'am, I don't. You're, Anne, right?"

She covered her gaping mouth with her hand. "You

know my name. How?"

"It's a long story, Anne. And I'm afraid I don't have the time to tell it."

"Come on in, boy. Ain't gonna bite ya'," she said and picked up the knife.

She walked up the steps and into the trailer.

Stephen followed her.

Empty bottles of whiskey and newspapers littered the inside. Playing cards and lottery tickets covered the table. Brown shag carpet squished beneath his feet. Dirty dishes filled the sorry excuse for a sink. It reeked of cigarettes and baby food. He saw a Birthday card lying on the table.

She walked around the table and sat, motioning for him to do the same.

Stephen joined her.

"How's about tellin' me how you got here, hmm?"

"I came here for my daughter."

"You said that." She placed her elbow on the table and rested her head in her hand. "I want to know *how* you did it."

"How do I know you're not Darrell?" Stephen said.

"Darrell!" she said, and pulled out the knife so fast, Stephen couldn't react until the point touched his throat. "He sent you?"

Commands from his brain failed. A cold paralysis set in.

"No, Ma'am. And I think it's a safe bet to say we're on the same side."

"Ain't movin' the knife 'til I get my answers."

Stephen's eye twitched as sweat dripped in it, giving everything a fish-eye perspective.

Don't move.

She moved the tip of the knife up his neck and then his cheek resting it just below his eyeball.

"I have help...my wife, she's a nurse. She put me in a

coma. I don't know how much time I've got left."

"I'd say so! 'Specially," she said, tracing the tip of the blade to the corner of his eye, "if you won't tell me *how* you got here."

Stephen's bladder emptied. The warmth spread from his crotch to his ass.

"Darrell ran into us with his ice cream truck. My daughter, Allyson, died. Me? It just took my arm."

She removed the knife from his face, lay in on the table and sat across from him. She wrung her hands.

"But you didn't lose ya' arm. I can see it!"

"I...I'm not disagreeing, but, yes, it sheared it off at the shoulder. Here," Stephen pointed to the long scar that started at the top his right shoulder and ran down to his nipple, "see?"

She squinted at it. "Mind if I touch it?"

"Go ahead."

What did Darrell do to you, Anne?

She reached across the small table and traced the scar with her finger. "Must'a hurt like a son-of-a-bitch."

"Not as much as losing my daughter. Nowhere close."

"Trust me, Sugar, I know exactly what we're talkin' 'bout," Anne said, moving a stray lock of hair from her eye.

"You have a daughter too, right?"

"Sarah. She'd be five-years-old...hell, I can't count the days here. But, before Darrell ran us over, she would'a been five." She took a deep breath as she ran her fingers through her black hair. Tears began to pat on the small table. "Whadd'a say your name was?"

"Stephen. Stephen Morrison."

"Well, Stephen, I got some *real* bad news for ya,'" she wiped away her tears, "Ya' daughter's dead. You ain't savin' her. This is *his* world, now."

"I know she's dead. I just...I'm here to get her out. Is that possible?"

"Sugar, you need to listen, and listen good. Ya' listenin'?"

Stephen bit down on his lower lip, cursing himself for not bringing his handgun.

"Yes."

"We lost Sarah in a car accident, too." Anne picked up an old newspaper and began pulling strips of it apart. "Darrell went crazy after that. He hired a psychic, paranormalists, the whole nine yards."

Anne wadded up the paper she ripped, and began tearing a fresh page.

"But after he started readin' them books...he got *real* bad. I'll never forget that day. I was sitting outside in our backyard , and he rushes out saying 'If ya' want something done right, you gotta do it on your own.' Said everythin' he read was hogwash. Said he found a way to get back our daughter Sarah back."

She tossed the paper aside in favor of a magazine.

"I told him he was crazy. He yokes me up, hauls me inside, and shows me a map. Pointed where the accident happened, and said we got lucky."

"Lucky?" Stephen clung to every word, the reality of it so familiar it made him shiver.

"Said all it would take would be a few more deaths, something about how many people died there, and how it was fit to burst and, if he found the right vehicle, he could find her." She motioned with her hands, her eyes searching the small room.

"I thought he, well, just had an episode, or somethin.' But... as the days passed, he stopped bathing, wouldn't even wash his hands. And when he came home reeking of blood, long story short, I told him I was gone. I can't condone *murderin'* people. He threatened me a fate worse than death. He made good on his promise." Her eyes scanned the dilapidated trailer.

"Do you see Sarah?" Stephen asked.

Anne crossed her arms and pursed her lips. "Only when he drives by in that stupid ice cream truck of his. Circles 'round, blarin' that god-awful horn. I can't look at her no more. She's...changed. But every time he drives by with her, I *can't* help but look. That make sense?"

"Anne, trust me, I've had to swallow a lot of...interesting things recently."

"Swallow this: If you think for a minute you're gonna just up and come in here," she laughed so hard, she began to cough. "No offense, but you're fucked. Got me?"

"I'm sorry, I don't."

"You may be able to *see* your daughter, but...there's no leavin' here. Ya' wife may be able to pull you out that coma, but your daughter is here forever...like my little angel, Sarah."

"I have a plan." He raised his ethereal arm and rested it on the table. "Darrell has used it to kill my brother, his children, and his wife. I want to see what it can do here."

"Honey, the only reason why ya' arm is glowin' is 'cause you can't let go of ya' daughter. That's all it is, Sugar. I'm sorry to tell ya' this, Mr. Morrison, but that's all ya' arm is good for. Jack shit."

Stephen wanted out. Out of everything. The casino had spoken, and the house always wins.

"But I felt—"

"Screw what ya' felt. Let me put it in simple terms. As soon as you let go of your daughter, you know, the emotions, it'll fade. Or, if he gets to her before you do, and does what he did to Sarah, well, it'll vanish just the same."

"No...I don't...I don't believe that. I'm not some random jerk-off. He picked me for a reason, and I'll find a way to use it!"

A pressure squeezed at Stephen's heart. Energy surged up and down his arm. He felt like he was underwater again.

"Sugar, you okay?"

"No," he said, rubbing his head. "I keep getting this feeling like I'm underwater."

"Funny. That's how I felt after comin' here. You sayin' you felt that *before* you came here?"

They found Darrell's apartment flooded.

"Yeah, what does that mean?"

"You got me. My guess is Darrell's afraid of it. This place, it's brings out the worst in you, the darkest part. Your worst fears."

Darrell's afraid of water... But where can I find water here?

"Seein' is believin' honey. It went away when he turned Sarah with her Birthday present...that damned crayon. Warps ya' mind."

"What was it?"

"Once the emotions die, or he gets to her, it's over. He wins. This...world he created—damn me for not sayin' anythin' earlier 'bout those damn books he was readin.' Shoulda' known."

Stephen leaned in close to Anne. "I have to try, Anne. I. Am. Saving. My. Daughter."

"I won't let ya.'"

"What?"

"You go up there all half-cocked, he'll use that arm to do what he's been tryin' to do since he got here."

"What's he trying to do?"

"Stay here in this messed up Candy Land he created and burn everything else. Worlds, even. It's Darrell's world now. We're just livin' in it."

"Is...is Allie with him?"

"Stay here with me, Sugar. You have no idea how lonely I am. I'm nice, once you get to know me." Anne reached a hand across the table , "Hate to tell ya', but we've been playin' poker since ya' got here, and I got me a full house. I call, Mr. Morrison. He *wants* you to go down there."

Stephen registered the flash of the knife as soon as its point entered his throat.

"Ain't lettin' you help him. Ya' understand?" she said, teasing the point of the knife in and out of the small wound. The tip of her tongue licked her lips as she concentrated. "Trust me. It's for the best."

Stephen felt for the pen in a world that was a million miles away. He scribbled as fast as he could: *Anne! Help!*

"Anne, what if I could save your daughter?" Stephen said.

Anne cocked her head, inserting the blade farther.

Stephen tried to swallow but there was no room. He tilted his head back as far as he could.

The pressure of the dull knife separated his flesh in a little, jagged L. It didn't feel like a knife, more like a pair of needle nose pliers jabbing inside, pinching, wrenching.

"Told ya.' I call, and I got me a full house. You'd do the same for your daughter."

"I lied! I lied, okay?"

Anne's face reminded him of his kindergarten teacher when she caught him eating the crayons.

"Go on," Anne said.

"I'm here for both of our daughters. I *can* save them."

Laughter erupted from Anne like a geyser. She slammed her hand on the table, scattering lottery tickets and playing cards.

"I may be from the country, but that don't mean I'm stupid. You're an errand boy, come to collect somethin' that don't exist."

Please work. Please work. Please work.

"Then how did I get your daughter here? She's staring at you through the window." Stephen pointed over her shoulder.

Anne turned her head, keeping one eye on him.

It'll have to do.

Stephen grabbed the hand holding the knife and pushed the blade out. Warm blood trickled down from the wound.

Anne swung at him with an ashtray, missing the side of his head by an inch.

Stephen stood, holding her arm with the knife mere inches from his face.

She threw another ashtray and clipped his forehead.

A kaleidoscope spun in front of his eyes.

Don't faint. Be strong for Allie.

Stephen let go of Anne and turned toward the door.

Hot iron sank into his back between his ribs.

The kaleidoscope spun faster. Liquid slowly filled his right lung.

"Goddammit, stand still!" Anne said, pulling the blade from his back to strike again.

Stephen fell forward and tumbled down the steps. He landed on his back, knocking the air out of his lungs. Blood filled his mouth.

"Come here!" Anne scrambled down the steps.

Stephen skittered backward, digging into the ground and pushing with his heels.

Move! Move! Move!

Anne leaped at him, holding the knife with both hands.

Stephen rolled over, and over, and over, placing as much distance between them as he could.

"You ain't takin' my Sarah, no, sir."

Stephen rolled onto his stomach, brought his knees to his chest and pushed with his hand.

The knife hit the bone in his forearm. He fell backward just beyond the dome.

Stephen placed his hand on his knee and lowered his head, taking in deep breaths.

He reached for the pen again, and wrote: *Almost there.*

He felt Shelley's hand cover his.

Anne dropped the knife and beat on the dome with her fists.

"It's what he *wants* you to do! Can't ya' see that?"

Stephen ran toward The Lost Ones surrounding Allie.

Chapter 16

Stephen made his way through the deadfall, shaking off countless bugs and creatures that scoured him, seeking his mouth, his nose. As he came to the bottom of the hill, the tip of the pyre The Lost Ones were dancing around grew brighter, and the smell of freshly cooked veal called to him.

His feet barely kept their balance as he climbed. When he crested the hill, he saw the same glow that had greeted him when he entered this world. As he walked down, he saw the fire that burned like the flame of a Zippo in the wind and the train's derailed cars that encircled it. Shadows of The Lost Ones danced across the boughs of the trees above and stretched across the scorched land like Halloween decorations.

Before he made his way down, he noticed how far his arm had faded. How slow his heartbeat was. How little of the wind his body allowed inside. Stephen felt for the pen again, and flipped a page with fingers that labored to do so, and wrote: *Time?* He felt a faint hand grasp his, squeezing four digits. *Four.* Four minutes there.

Here?

He wanted to scream Allie's name. Just stand up and scream it while flapping his arms like he did as a child with his Superman cape on. Something snatched him like an alligator does a thirsty dog that wanders too close to the lip of the lake, and pulled him down. The Lost Ones.

Invisible strings lifted and pulled him through the air, like a marionette controlled by a child...

Or Darrell...

Whoever controlled him let go as soon as he was above them. He landed on his ass, jarring his spine. Fire crackled in front of the patch of dirt where he landed. Little orange and red embers drifted into the air and were pushed back down as if blown by a mouth.

The woman sitting to his left wore a dress only death and time could tatter. The top of her head and the side of her face were aflame. The flames didn't dance or crackle. Like a Polaroid, or a film stuck on pause, they were still. Only a thin line of smoke wavered in the breeze.

A small boy sat next to her, swaying back and forth with the rhythm and whim of the night. The scamp raised his arms. The poor thing's tongue dangled where the lower jaw should be. The point of his tongue had long been withered away. Bone-white worms burst from the organ, only to curl back into a perfect circle where its mandibles started burrowing another hole for their glistening, throbbing bodies to enter and spill its eggs.

A headless man wearing faded bib overalls poked the fire with a stick. A woman with the better part of a seat from the train jutting from her chest snuggled up to a little girl whose eyes were sewn shut.

Someone had erected crude stick figures made of tree branches and clothed in burlap and whatever clothes they could spare. Effigies of those they remembered. The burlap sacks on their heads had crudely stitched X's for eyes, and jagged smiles sealed with more X's. They swayed outside the circle near the busted railcars.

A small boy tossed a weathered baseball at one of them, waiting for it to throw it back. They were trapped in time. Trapped in space and the fleeting moments of memories that blew in the wind like dead leaves in winter.

A shadow darted from the nearest railcar. A giggle echoed. The quick shuffling of footsteps. A small, pallid face peaked at him from behind the headless man.

The little girl leaped out from behind him and pounced on the girl whose eyes and mouth were sewn shut. She wore a dark dress covered in spider webs. Her black hair was pulled back and braided. When Stephen focused on it, he could see her hair as it shifted, crawled. A few of the larger spiders climbed down and fretted about her white, blood stained face. But her teeth... The campfire gave the rows of barbed wire a rusted hue. She sat atop her, holding something in her hand that was pointed down.

Stephen's heart raced, his sight coming and going with each pump.

"Hold still! I'm trying to help you *see!*" She pried the girl's hands away from her eyes. "It'll only hurt for a minute. You're no fun to play with without eyes!"

She brought the black crayon down and it sounded like bubble-wrap popping. The poor thing tried to wail but her stitches confined the sound to her throat.

Stephen shuddered, and wondered whether he—or Allie—would be next.

She pulled the crayon out and began scribbling in and around her sockets. Like a black mist, the color hung above her face and squiggled. Squiggled like...

Darrell.

"See? Now ain't that better?" the little psychopath let her up. Even the stitches across her lips couldn't contain the mewling from the eyeless girl.

Focus! Focus!

He looked at the faded blue of his arm and wiggled his fingers until they caught the pen. They felt as if they were asleep. He wrote: *Time?* And felt three fingers squeeze together.

Only three?

Out of the corner of his eye, he saw a yellow pig-tail bounce up and down inside the nearest railcar.

"Allie? Allie-bear?" he said, coughing up blood and tissue. It sounded like a tree frog hitting the ground when he spat. He took a deep breath and felt the onset of dizziness.

I gotta slow down...for her. I've still got one lung. Deep breaths.

He stood, knees popping.

The Lost Ones' eyes found him. When they stood as well, he heard creaks and branches breaking.

The woman with her head aflame reached out and grabbed his wrist with a hand as mushy as fungus.

"Don't give him what he wants! Don't you *dare!*" She reached for his face. Her fingernails long gone, reduced to rips of flesh running up to her knuckles.

Stephen pulled away and shrieked when her hand detached from her body. Her grip tightened until his fingers felt like they were going to burst. He clawed at the digits with his ghostly appendage. The skin sloughed off like mold from bread.

Stephen ran for the railcar Allie was hiding in.

He slammed his hand against the side of the railcar. The bones of the lady's hand broke like dry twigs. Her hand fell to the ground and twitched like it was hit with voltage until the ground sucked it down.

Stephen pulled at the railcar's door when he felt the hands from The Lost Ones come down on him. A fleshless hand clawed into his back and found the wound. Something soft and squishy pushed its way inside. Its fingernails dug in, separating skin from muscle. A hard object hit the back of his head. Different colored flashes went off behind his eyes. Double vision replaced clarity.

"Allie! Baby! It's your Daddy! Open up!"

For a brief moment, he heard her voice. That sweet song at the center of his heart that resonated through his body, warming it, filling it up. His arm grew brighter.

"Daddy!"

"Hold on, Sweetie. There we go. Now hold on."

He turned and blindly swung his fist. The first person he hit felt like a rotten pumpkin. As his arm sank down in the mess, more hands tore at his back. A tree branch whacked the side of his head. A warm, little river trickled down.

"Allie! I'm comin', Baby."

Stephen pulled on the bar with both hands, mustering every ounce of energy he had. His shoulders threatened to separate when he felt the rusted door slide a few inches. The sound of nails across chalkboards filled his ears. He gave another yank and forced himself in sideways to avoid any more blows. The space wasn't big enough.

Stephen took a deep breath. Planted his hands on the doorway and pushed with his back until he felt a disc slip. Plucking his spine like a heated guitar string.

"Fuck!"

He pushed again and then slid in, yanking the door shut behind him.

Allie wore the dress Shelley made for her on her fourth birthday: the blue and white one with kittens chasing yarn. Her hair was in pigtails—just how she always wanted it. Eyes the color of an August sky—not crayon-black—swelled at the sight of her father. She ran toward him, arms outstretched and stopped, her mouth making a large O.

"No, you'll hurt me!" she screamed and cowered into the back of the railcar, hiding behind a seat. Her little fingers dug into the top, turning white.

"Come on now, Baby, we have to get you out of here."

"No! You're the bad man!"

"He's not here, Sweetie. Please, just give Daddy a hug, okay? Daddy *and* Mommy miss you more than you can possibly imagine." Stephen broke into a sob that quaked his body. "*Please,* Baby, let's go."

The top of Allie's face peaked above the seat and

regarded him.

"Go where?"

"Well, we'll go where I came in from. Mommy will wake me up, and I'll be holding onto you *so* tight with my arm, Baby. We have to try, Allie."

Allie pointed just beyond him. He swallowed hard and turned his head. Outside, a wind howled and shook the railcar, tossing The Lost Ones around like ragdolls. Heads and limbs broke off, striking and cracking the windows. Ruby-red embers from the fire swirled in the chaos. They lingered like cigarette butts striking asphalt.

Stephen ran to her, to his Allie-bear, and when he kneeled down to shield her, his senses flooded with the lavender smell of her hair, the feel of it through his fingers. He kissed her cheek and tasted a hint of peanut butter and jelly.

For the first time in what felt like a million years, Stephen embraced his daughter. All he could do was sit there and hold her, caress her. The pain, the memories, fell away like an avalanche. Stephen could almost smell Shelley cooking Allie's favorite pancakes, as if none of this horrible mess had happened.

"Allie, take my hand, Bugga-boo."

Stephen reached out for a pen and wrote: *Touch my hand.*

A faint, but warm hand took his from home.

Allie reached out and placed her hand atop theirs.

"Mommy!" She said. Her Carribean-blue eyes grew brighter, and for just a moment, Stephen could see Allie the way she was. The way she should be. The way *they* should be.

Shelley's grip tightened. Tears pattered on his—*their* hand.

Our hand?

A deafening boom shook the railcar as something large

collided with it. Allie scurried to the back of the railcar, and Stephen followed.

"I love you so *much*, Allie-bear. Whatever happens, Baby...Mommy and Daddy miss you so much, Bug-a-boo."

"I miss Mommy. I wanna go home."

"I know, Baby. We'll find a way."

Allie stared at his blue arm and reached out to touch it, but drew away. Her little face twisted with scorn.

"That," she said and pointed at his arm as she backed away from him, "is that an ouchie?"

"Yeah," Stephen chuckled. "You could call it that."

A familiar scream filled the antiquated car. Another window burst, showering them with tiny, invisible razors. A few nipped Stephen's cheek, his neck, loosing warm culverts.

"Stephen!" Josh yelled.

Like the space shuttle entering the atmosphere, another boom shook the ground. The railcar tilted and whined on rusted wheels. Other cars followed in line and were placed carefully back on the wounded track as it repaired itself.

"Allie, we have to get you out of here, Baby."

"I wanna go home!"

Stephen wiggled his fingers until he felt the pen—a pen that his fingers almost passed through—and wrote: *Time?* The tips of two fingers tingled, the warmth scarce. Two minutes.

"We're getting out of here, Baby. But we don't have much time."

A familiar childhood melody carried across the air. The piano sounded as if a slab of concrete lay across its strings. Its hammers were just metal; the pads eaten by a shadow from a place between the stars. Like everything else here, it was deranged; playing backwards, and underwater. Stephen's sweat froze.

All of the color drained from Allie's face. Stephen felt

the moisture from her gasp on his face.

Its headlights blinded them as Darrell pulled up to the railcar. He honked the horn three times. Its engine shut off. Then a door slammed.

"All aboard!" Darrell smiled at them. Endless rows of jagged ivory ran all the way down his throat, glistening below eyes that spewed fire. Galaxies spun inside, hypnotizing Stephen, begging him to stay a *little* while longer. A putrid smell overcame him as Darrell moved closer—his cracked grin spattering black pools on the once vibrant red carpet. "Sarah, come on in, Sugar-pie."

"Stay away from us!" Stephen wedged Allie up against the wall. She squirmed behind him. "I don't care what you want to do with me, just please, let Allie go."

Please think I'm dead. Please think I'm dead.

A laugh that hummed like a fly in a spider's web echoed off the walls as the grin became larger, the calderas in his sockets brighter. Little Sarah peeked her head from behind her father. Her pale, cracked face reminded Stephen of dolls from garage sales. Ones that were handed down for generations. Possibly more. Black lips curled a smile, fracturing the cracks farther until they oozed a thick, pungent oil Stephen could almost taste. He wretched.

"I wannna play with her, Daddy!"

"How 'bout that? Why don't we let 'em play, Hoss?"

"Let us go!"

"Not yet, Stevie." Darrell reached down, placing his hand on Stephen's shoulder. "I ain't had the chance to thank you."

Don't be like your father. Control your emotions.

"Thank me? For what?"

"For finally killin' yourself. You're my anchor, Hoss. Without you, my daughter wouldn't have someone to play with, and I wouldn't have you now, would I?"

So far, so good.

"What's so special about me?"

Darrell's fingers cinched down on Stephen's collar bone until it snapped.

Allie jumped when he shrieked.

Little Sarah, at Darrell's side, watched and waited with a switchblade smile on her lips.

"There, Lil' Miss is. Saw her across the street before I came through the light and pointed my truck at ya.' I knew they'd get along just fine. But that face you made when you saw me comin,' Man, wish I'd had a camera!"

Every second of the wreck. Every nightmare of Allie being taken away—and that feeling—that feeling of small digits clinging to his finger.

"I want to play, Daddy!" Sarah's voice buzzed like a bumble bee.

Darrell took a step forward, examining his fingernails. "This is the part where I say: Difference between you and me ain't that much. You know that? Look how far I went to get what I wanted. Now...look at you, Hoss."

"Fuck you!"

Control your emotions!

"Now, now, where's your manners? Contrary to what you *may* believe, I like you Stevie. You're a hell of a guy. Worlds are about to burn, and I'm offering you a front row seat to the end of everything I despise, and this is how you act?" Darrell winked at him. "You just sit there, yes, sir. You sit there and enjoy your little family reunion. Never cared for the rain that much, anyway. I got fireworks to light!"

What did he just say?

Darrell let go of him. He walked to the open door of the railcar and surveyed the incomplete bodies searching for their heads, their arms, their legs.

The flaming woman's son picked up his head and tried to place it atop his shoulders again. His tongue hung down while little, red spiders spilled from it.

Sarah moved closer to Stephen, to Allie.

She pulled a black crayon from inside her black dress. "This is my Birthday present from Daddy. It helps you see what's *really* here," Sarah pointed to a window, "what's out there, too. It'll change you...it's not *that* bad."

"I said: All aboard! Come on now, we ain't got all day." Darrell struck a match. He tossed it outside and spat on it. Flames engulfed the ground.

Some of The Lost Ones caught fire and screamed. They ran in circles, bumping into one another. Eyes popped like champagne corks. The smell of rot and burning rubber wafted inside the railcar.

Stephen covered his mouth with his hand, trying to hold the vomit back. He remembered the war stories he heard from vets: *"It's a smell you'll never get out of your nose."*

The fire burned through the ground, dripping onto the street of the real world below. Darrell laughed and tossed another match.

"Allie, that's her name, ain't it, bud? You got a pet-name for her, dontcha'? Hmmm? Prolly something *queer* like, *Princess*....innit?"

Stephen felt an anger he hadn't felt since he watched his father beat his mother. Cold beads of sweat turned hot and came out of every pore in his body. His lip twitched, and turned into a snarl. Shining, blue current set his arm ablaze. He looked into Darrell's eyes and saw his father.

Stephen rushed to Darrell like a feral animal—forgetting his back that screamed with fire—and swung wild.

Darrell caught his fist and snarled, grinding his teeth. The sound was like a chair dragged across a hardwood floor. The furnaces in Darrell's eyes grew, spinning faster.

Stephen could feel the heat from them on his face. The smell of burning hair made him pull his head back.

Darrell wagged a finger at him, squeezed and pulled Stephen toward him.

"Hold still!" Sarah said, "I want you to see what *I* see!"

"Allie!" Stephen screamed. He twisted his head.

Allie kicked the little devil.

Darrell spat on Stephen's face and pulled him close. "Do not fuck with me, little man. We ain't done just yet. You gonna play nice?"

Rotten fish raced up Stephen's sinuses as Darrell lifted him off the ground and pulled him so close their noses touched.

"Yes!"

"Good! Sarah, Honey, let that little princess *see!*"

Stephen's shoulder separated. He wailed.

Allie-bear cried out, again.

Darrell cupped his hands around his mouth. "Sit back, enjoy the ride, and let the kids play," he whispered.

Stephen fell to the floor in a crumpled mess, his wounds crying out in unison. The world began to spin.

The Lost Ones—the ones that Darrell didn't burn—shambled down the aisle and filled up the seats.

Josh was the last one in line.

Darrell pulled him aside and pointed at Stephen.

"My father used to have a sayin': Can't spell families without lies! Right, Tubby?"

Josh nodded and walked back toward Stephen. He sat right across the aisle from him, unable to face him.

Lies?

"Daddy!" Allie called.

Stephen looked at his arm. The blue outline was gone. But, he forgot the pain—pushed it aside with all the other emotions that he capped inside of a bomb about to blow—and turned to Allie.

Allie had a piece of old and tattered wood. She swung it at Sarah, but missed. Her eyes found his, pleading.

Stephen took a deep breath and wiggled his ethereal fingers. Electricity surged up and down them, glowing a gentle blue like the bottom of a lighter's flame.

Stephen reached up and grabbed the side of a seat, withered and worn, and pulled himself up. He limped down the aisle, toward Darrell. Stephen balled up his hand—feeling the current—and struck.

Again, Darrell caught it. "What'choo gonna do, little faggot? Huh? Come on. Come on!" He grabbed Stephen's throat. Darrell forced his forearm inside Stephen's blue one. They seamlessly became one. For the first time since the accident, Stephen's arm felt real. Darrell's faint heart-beat pushed dead, old blood through his—their arm. "Now that's a plum better. Wait...is that a pen I feel? Hmm... Somebody's down there, ain't they?"

What's happening to me?

"Fuck you!"

"Oh, don't be so cantankerous. 'Sides, I wouldn't be talking that way. Now, let me take a guess...it's that *pretty* wife of yours...ain't it? She's good stock, I'll give you that. But she's got a mouth on her! Whoo, Boy!"

Stephen blinked the sweat out of his eyes and tried to pull his arm back.

"It *is* your wife, isn't it? Well...How 'bout I just reach out and touch someone!"

"No! No!"

"Then sit your ass *down!*"

Stephen did as he was told.

Darrell pulled his arm out of Stephen's ethereal one, breaking the intimacy. It felt like his arm was just pulled out of mud. Stephen wiggled the digits just to make sure it was his again.

He was a part of me. If I...

Stephen looked over his shoulder at Allie.

Sarah grabbed the piece of wood from Allie and cast it

aside. "Now..." Sarah touched the side of her head, making a bridge for the black widows to crawl across. When enough of them crawled onto her hand, she reached out to Allie. Venom dripped from their fangs, making little sizzling noises on the carpet. "Let me see your eyes."

"Do you want to know what I think?" Stephen said.

"Excuse me?'

"Did I stutter?"

"I'd sit down now. Before I have to really hurt ya.'"

"No. And you know *why* you won't."

Darrell reached for his throat.

Stephen grabbed his hand and pulled, but lost his balance.

Darrell stomped his stomach.

It knocked the wind out of Stephen. Spongy bits from his lungs blew out and sprayed Darrell's face.

What looked like the ebony head of a frog poked through Darrell's lips, shot out his tongue, and in three quick snaps devoured the morsels.

"You'll hurt me, but you won't kill me." Stephen smirked. "You can't. I'm already dead!"

Darrell groaned and reached for Stephen's throat. He missed, hitting the top of the seat.

Stephen looked out the window and watched the fragile moments that make up time skip by as the train edged forward.

Allie screamed out in pain.

"You hear that, Stevie? Hmmm? That's the sound I've been following ever since I lost *my* girl. These places... you're only limited by your imagination. It's just...possibilities, when it comes to the ever-after, here. And when you find yourself a place that's heavy, 'bout to burst, the possibilities are *limitless*. All you need is to pop it. Figure of speech."

"How?"

"Ah, hell. Forgot to thank you for this too," Darrell shrugged. "See, I tracked this kiddy-fiddler, and I lured him onto that road. Oh, he suffered, Hoss. Suffered things no man should see. Not because I hate kiddie-fiddlers, but his suffering had to be so bad, so *very* bad, to open up the crack, so I could find my daughter. Besides, I needed the wheels to go back and forth." Darrell patted Stephen on the head. "But now you're here, I've got something bigger, I've got a train. Now *that* can take a man places a truck can't! So, thanks, Stevie. Look, you keep your cool, and we'll see how this goes for ya.'"

The countless illuminated roads where The Lost Ones walked were vast, chasms where sounds, inhuman sounds, dictated the ebb and flow of time and the universes that spun from them. A euphoria that eclipsed his little blue and yellow pills hit him like the waves from his nightmares.

I'm not my father.

"I love you, Allie-bear!"

She's not screaming anymore...

Darrell pointed at the window. "What do ya' see?"

Stephen watched as the train slid along the silvery web, edging closer and closer to a sweet gravity that lulled him into a vast, warm and placid ocean. His body went numb. His wounds were silenced and replaced by something no drug could offer. Time slowed like the blood in Darrell's veins.

Control it. Don't let go. Don't let go.

"There you go, Hoss! Now you see what I'm talkin' about."

The train's engines came to life and screamed, splitting the night, shaking the walls and the ground. Acrid smoke entered from the broken window and burned his eyes.

"You just chew on that feelin' for a while, Hoss," Darrell said with a chuckle. "It's eternal. And you chew on the thought of ya' daughter never having to grow up, never having to be anything but your little girl. Your pills? Where we're headed...that tiny mind of yours...it'd burst! But I know the real reason you came up here. Let me help you."

Darrell's spittle landed on Stephen's face in slow motion. Stephen's grip loosened as the spots danced in front of his eyes.

If I'm not my father. I have to at least try.

Stephen thought of Allie, of Shelley, feeling the energy in his shared arm grow. He reached out and felt for the pen and grabbed it. He wrote: *No water. Drown me. For Allie.*

Stephen felt Shelley slap his hand in another world. He wrote back: *2 min. We're dead.*

What felt like an eternity passed as Stephen waited for her response. Finally, he felt her hand grab his and squeeze. This time, it was wet. Wet with tears. She moved the pen, spelling: U BLOOD OUT. Then, she made a heart symbol. He wrote back: *Wait till we're 1.* And placed a heart symbol below it.

God, I hope I'm right.

"Here, Hoss," Darrell pointed outside the window. "Death...death is just a dream. If ya' ask me, here's a much fairer hand that's dealt as opposed to what any of the world's bullshit religions says is...and should be. We've both seen what the world can do. This, this is a shortcut to forever. So, if you just calm down, I'll show you the way the world should be."

How do I get him to connect?

"I think you've fucked kids. You probably have a little fun with Sarah every night, you inbred, hillbilly, FUCK FACE!"

"Looks like you just chose the hard way. Well, I'll oblige."

Darrell slid his arm back inside Stephen's.

Stephen felt his fingers wiggle and flex into a fist. Dead blood flowed through his veins. He felt his hand grab the pen. Stephen screamed, grabbing at Darrell's face. Two of his fingers dug into Darrell's cheek and ripped it open.

This can't fail...

Darrell body slammed him, landing on top.

Two of Stephen's ribs snapped and speared his other lung. What air was left came out in a whine. He tried to breathe, but he could only take in so much, as more liquid filled his lungs.

A gentle hand landed atop theirs, and in one, swift action, Darrell stabbed Shelley's hand in another world. Once. Twice.

"She's a right bitch, I tell ya' what."

Drown me before he kills you!

Stephen felt their hand let go of the pen, and reach upward. He felt Shelley's throat. Their fingers encircled it and squeezed.

Shelley's fingers tried to pull it away. She jerked her body back and forth.

"I could snap her neck right now. Snap it like it were a matchstick! All because you couldn't let go of your daughter. Been to some dark places, Stevie, my boy, but that funk you were in screamed to me up here louder than all the others. I knew you'd be the one; convince me to move forward. Fix things. The dynamic duo!"

"All of this—" Stephen coughed, bringing up more blood.

For Allie. Be strong for Allie.

"—if you change, then, does it matter?"

"Don't you want to get this moving, and *see*? That's ya' problem." Darrell wagged his finger at Stephen. "Once Sarah finishes helpin' ya' girly-girl, well, you'll see."

"And just what will I see, huh? What's so fuckin' important?"

"Hoss," Darrell said, leaning into Stephen as the calderas spewed their lava, "*I* made it so you see what the world really is. What people really are. What make a man kill another. Wars. The worst shit you can imagine. Shit that'll get ya' a one way ticket to Looney-Ville. In cold, hard terms, I give the truth. Unfiltered. Unrated. Facts are facts."

"Sick fuck!" Stephen managed as he felt fingers close around Shelley's neck .

"Let's finish her off."

Dunk me! Dunk me!

Stephen mustered a cough and blew more blood across Darrell's face.

Allie ran up the aisle past them. A trail of blood followed her. So did Sarah.

Below the crack in the sky, Stephen felt his head submerge in cool, soothing water. He tried to breathe, but couldn't. Out of instinct, he lurched forward, fighting a sweet embrace only drowning can give. A sweet embrace that fixed everything.

Now if only I can take him with me...

Stephen took a deep breath and felt water enter his lungs.

Darrell's face went slack. The fire in his sockets went out. Brown, human eyes replaced them.

Stephen grabbed the back of Darrell's head, pulling him forward.

"Stop! Stop this! Sarah!"

Stephen embraced him, pinning their arm between them.

Darrell head butted him. "Fuck you!"

Every sense grew dimmer, distant. Except his hold on Darrell.

Almost there.

Darrell wriggled a hand, then his arm free. He plunged his thumbs into Stephen's eyes, twisting turning.

Stephen screamed, feeling every nerve, every ligament connecting each eye rip, tear. Stephen's grip tightened with every sensation, as Darrell threw his weight to the left, to the right. Stephen's fingers punctured his skin. His fingernails sank into what felt like a dirty diaper.

"I will kill her if you don't let go!" Darrell said.

Stephen's fingertips found one of Darrell's ribs and latched on.

"She's fucking dead," Darrell said as water poured from his mouth.

Stephen coughed and realized...

"I've got her, Hoss. You're fuckin' done!"

In their hand, he felt the side of the tub as Darrell pulled them out of the water. Then he felt them grab an arm. Shelley's arm. He pulled as hard as he could.

Stephen felt himself fall back into the tub. He dug into Darrell's back until he latched on to three ribs. He pulled, squeezed.

Shelley? Shell? Love?

"Poor thing's head hit the wall and fell in," Darrell said, "I didn't think you had the balls or the brains, Hoss. But it's your own fault. If only you would just see."

Stephen took another deep breath, filling his lungs.

"Daddy!" Allie screamed.

Come on you cocksucker. Die! Just. Fucking. DIE!

Stephen felt their hand reach up and try to grab the edge of the tub, but something...

Shell!

Pushed them back into the water.

Darrell's hand went to his neck as water poured from every orifice.

Stephen's senses dulled, and his grip faded.

The train shuddered as it came to a stop, right at the edge of land above the crack in the sky.

Josh charged toward them like he was holding a spear. He swung the broken table leg and smashed the back of Darrell's head. Cold droplets splattered Stephen's face.

This is it. I'm—we're dead.

Black invaded Darrell's once blue veins and raced up

his arm to his face. His eyes twitched as water swelled them. He reminded Stephen of a cat trying to hack up a fur ball.

The faint embers in Darrell's sockets died. Only smoke drifted out, forming ash-gray clouds that hung above his head like fog above a street on a hot day.

Darrell's body became wet, brown sand, like a crude sandcastle a child had made at the beach. A beach that was pummeled by a hurricane, as it pulled the grains of Darrell into its swirling vortex. What used to be a little girl with spiders for hair and barbwire for teeth stopped mid-stride and turned to ash. The last vestiges of the storm pulled her away, starting with her head, and working its way down.

Both disappeared.

You were right, Darrell. You're only limited by your imagination.

Stephen felt the last of his consciousness drift away like a tumbleweed until...

~

...it came back.

Stephen took an enormous gulp for air. Then, he realized he didn't have to. This was a high he had never felt. A solace only dreams could create: Freedom. He leaned his head back and smiled. For the first time in his life, Stephen was proud.

The Lost Ones began to glow blue and ascend. Higher and higher they went, reassembling themselves. The fire that consumed the woman's head was gone. Her face was whole, her hair bouncing with the breeze. The little boy's mouth was fixed. As they spun around each other, she reached out and embraced him. For the first time in over a hundred years, she kissed her son.

I know how it feels...

"Allie?" Stephen said.

"Daddy!" Allie yelled.

Stephen raised his ethereal appendage. "Come here, Baby."

Little tears pattered the floor as she jumped up and down, her golden hair bouncing above those azure eyes.

Blue...still blue.

"Take my hand," Stephen said.

Allyson's little hand grabbed his and squeezed. The other touched his face. Stephen remembered carrying Allie on his shoulders at the beach. The first time they went snorkeling; her first word; being the first to hold her at the hospital after she was born. And how that little hand had latched onto his pinky and squeezed.

"Please don't leave me again, Daddy."

"Don't worry, Allie-bear. Just hold on tight, okay?"

Allie embraced him and held on tight.

Josh knelt beside them and did the same.

Stephen looked upward and saw a light brighter than the sun, brighter than Allie.

They floated like lightning bugs on an August night.

"Look, Daddy!"

Stephen looked down and watched as the molten-pewter clouds swirled, faster and faster. Like dirty water down a drain, they carried what Darrell had created away, sealing the crack in the sky as if it were repairing a crack in a windshield.

"Daddy?"

"Yes, Bugga-boo?"

"Can we go scuba diving there?" she asked and pointed upward, and beyond to one of the spinning galaxies among myriad others.

Stephen followed her gaze to a little spiral hanging in the darkness of space, and saw everything clearly.

Shelley waved at them, with the ocean behind her, as she walked along the beach.

He watched the wave come in and break as families played with their children. A dog ran by, barking at a little boy who refused to throw the Frisbee again.

"Sure, Baby. Anything you want...anything."

Acknowledgments

Special thanks to my beta-readers: Patrick Rutigliano, Anthony J. Rapino, Sheldon Higdon, Dylan J. Morgan, Lisa Jenkins, and Mary Rajotte.

Extra special thanks to Kate Jonez. To write is human, to edit is divine. You were divine.

About the Author

Ben Eads lives within the semi-tropical suburbs of Central Florida. A true horror writer by heart, he wrote his first story at the tender age of ten. The look on the teacher's face when she read it was priceless. However, his classmates loved it! Ben has had short stories published in various magazines and anthologies. When he isn't writing, he dabbles in martial arts, philosophy and specializes in I.T. security. He's always looking to find new ways to infect reader's imaginations. Ben blames Arthur Machen, H.P. Lovecraft, Jorge Luis Borges, J.G. Ballard, Philip K. Dick, and Stephen King for his addiction, and his need to push the envelope of fiction. For more information, please visit www.beneadsfiction.com.

Made in the USA
Middletown, DE
01 April 2015